RED INDIAN

The Final Days

TERRY FOSS

Published by: Fossil

4 Harvard Drive

Mount Pearl, Newfoundland and Labrador,

Canada

A1N 2Z7

ISBN 978-0-9940209-2-5

Published March 2016

Printed in United States

Edited by: Julieanne Reddy

Cover Art: Claude Randell

Dedication

This book is dedicated to my wife Sharon, whose daily struggle, in the face of the daunting odds mounted against her by the insidious disease of MS, is nothing short of heroic.

We have traces enough left only to cause our sorrow that so peculiar and so superior a people should have disappeared from the earth like a shadow.

William Epps Cormack

Preface

It is the year 1823. The Beothuk nation, estimated to have reached eight to ten thousand at its peak, have now been reduced to fifteen. To say their future is bleak at this point is little more than stating the obvious. Yet in their world, survival is what they must strive for. They have families to provide for, children to love, and lives to live.

Many forces conspired to bring them to this point, but arguably the most damaging was the arrival of the Europeans to the island. Two distinctively different cultures were vying for the same land and the resources it had to give.

Although the Beothuk had strength of family and community, the new settlers had strength of numbers and technology. It was a challenge the Red Indians were unequipped to win.

In the first book of this series I introduced you to the family of Shanawdithit. We travelled with them, sharing their struggles and their joys, from the time her mother Shanadee was a young girl to the day when Shanawdithit and her two companions were banished from their camp.

This book will tell the stories of the fifteen that remained.

Terry's Books

Through Beothuk Land

Holmes

Beothuk Slaves

Bloody Point

Red Indian - The Beginning

Red Indian - The Final Days

Red Indian - The Early Years

Chapter 1

1823

Jaywritt shifted his weight yet again in his unending search for a more comfortable seat on the cold, snow-covered boulder. With its natural flat top, it appeared as if Mother Earth had placed it there solely for his sitting pleasure; but in all the times he had used it before, he had yet to find the elusive comfortable spot. He had built his mamateek just behind the boulder so it sat strategically just outside the door. He was not sure why he had chosen that spot but it seemed to be a good idea at the time. But then, it wasn't the first time in his thirty-nine years he had made a decision that left him scratching his head, wondering why he had done it in the first place; and it probably wouldn't be the last.

He had gotten heavier these last few years, a little thicker around the waist. He had always been chubby as a boy, and even though he had thinned out in the years before he had grown into a man, his body had recently found its way back to his boyhood form. He wasn't sure if it was the cold boulder or the extra weight, but his legs were numb. He shifted again.

His hunting weapons were scattered around his feet in the trampled snow. His hathemay (bow) lay atop the birch quiver from which some of his newly finished arrows were spilling out. The arrow tips he had shaped from some pieces of iron that he had taken from a settler's shed earlier this year. Shaping them had been no easy task. Long hours of burning them in the fire pit and hammering them with the back of his hatchet had been followed with even more days of sharpening the edges with river stones; like he was now doing with his knife. There must be a better way, he thought. If only the Buggishaman (white man) used arrows; then I could use theirs. His eyes turned to the aaduth (sealing spear) lying on the snowy ground to his left. His son was born following a very successful sealing season, and like the spear he had used, he chose to name him Aaduth. Soon his son would be using his namesake to partake in the hunting season himself. This would be Aaduth's first trip to the coast, at least the first one he would remember. The last time he had been only an infant strapped to his mother's back; much too young to remember any of it. That was a good thing, Jaywritt thought. Those were horrible days, after my sister Shanadee was murdered. Better Aaduth was too young to remember any of it.

Stirred by the still fresh memories, the skinning knife that he was holding began to shake as his hand trembled. He steadied the knife in his hand as he continued running a flat beach stone over the edge of the blade, first one side then the other. Occasionally he spat on the stone's smooth surface to keep it slippery. Lifting the blade to eye level, he ran his eyes along its length and then tested his thumb on the edge. Still not satisfied, he continued to patiently draw the edge across the damp stone.

His mind wandered back in time as he worked; back to a time when he was much younger, a time when someone else carried the load of the tribe, a happier time. He thought of his sister Shanadee. He thought of her often these days, as he was forced into making decisions for the tribe on his own. He often wondered what she would do in the many situations he found himself. He did not have the strong personality and fierce determination his older sister had. He wished someone else were here to carry this load. Decisions did not come as easy to him.

He smiled softly as he remembered how Shanadee had relentlessly pushed him to practice with the hathemay, day after day until he was one of the best in the camp. He had never mastered the hathemay like she had, but he remembered seeing the sparkle of pride in her eyes the day his arrow split hers, finding the same spot on the birch target she had struck moments before. He had never been able to repeat that feat again, but he still remembered their excitement when it happened.

He had always been able to see the softer side of Shanadee; the side she had kept hidden from the rest of the tribe. He had only been five when his mother had been killed by the Buggishaman and Shanadee had cared for him after that. Many times he had fallen asleep to her soft singing as they lay alone in their mamateek with the dark, familiar forest wrapped protectively around them.

He missed his sister deeply. A part of him had died that day five years ago when Shanawdithit had stumbled into camp with the terrible news. Shanadee and the children with her had been slaughtered on the sea as Shanawdithit had helplessly watched from the cliff above. He had returned to that place many times since, but the only trace of his family was a broken hathemay that had washed up on the rocky beach. He knew it was his sister's because of the blue jay feather dangling from the end of one of the broken pieces. Now the broken hathemay was stored on a high shelf inside the mamateek.

The piercing shriek of a blue jay brought him back to the present. It was perched in the low branches of a tall birch tree that overhung one of the other two mamateeks in the clearing. Its shriek had also startled those inside.

"Stupid damn bird!" he heard old Jeddilledt mutter sleepily.

Inside he could hear the rustle of fur skins being pushed aside as they rolled out of bed. Jeddilledt was the oldest Beothuk in the camp; in fact, he was the oldest living Beothuk as far as Jaywritt knew. There were no other camps to be found around the Great

River. The tribe had dwindled down to the fifteen living in the three mamateeks here in this clearing.

He felt the weight return to his chest, like some giant hand squeezing his lungs. His breathing became shallow and he struggled to pull enough air into his starved lungs. Slipping from the boulder to his knees, he scooped a handful of snow and rubbed it over his face. The shock of the cold seemed to help.

Still on his hands and knees, he looked around the clearing. No one had seen him. That would be the last thing he needed.

He pushed himself to a sitting position and rested his back against the boulder. His breathing was settling down and his heart was no longer racing like a wounded rabbit. His body felt wet from inside his clothes and he shivered with the cold. These attacks were getting worse and he didn't know how to control it. He knew they were often triggered by the hopelessness he felt when he thought of the size of the tribe and the certainty that they would not survive. It was a weight that was too much for him to carry. His sister would have been better at this.

Behind him, the thick washawet (bear) skin was pushed aside and Aaduth stepped outside into the chilly morning air.

"Morning, Father", he smiled happily as he vigorously rubbed his hands together to warm them.

"I see you my son," Jaywritt replied.

The bold jay fluttered down to perch on a limb just behind Aaduth, causing the disturbed branch to shake and shed its covering of snow. Aaduth watched as it drifted through the air, sprinkling the ground below with a fresh dusting of white.

The jay sat there chastising them for not providing food.

"He's going to wake everyone in the camp," laughed Aaduth.

"I think he's already done that," replied Jaywritt. "I heard old Jeddilledt complaining a few minutes ago."

"Well if I were the jay, I'd be gone before he gets out here," snickered Aaduth.

"Probably a smart thing for him to do," agreed Jaywritt.

"Are you getting ready for our trip to the coast for the monau (seal) hunt?"

"Yes."

"Are we leaving soon?" he asked excitedly.

"Couple of days, maybe," smiled Jaywritt, noticing the shine of excitement in his son's eyes.

"I can't wait," blurted Aaduth as he shifted from one foot to the other.

"It's going to be a great trip. Now go gather some firewood for your mother while I finish sharpening my knife."

"Basadict!" Aaduth yelled loudly in the direction of Jeddilledt's mamateek. "Let's go."

Basadict's head peeked out around the caribou skin door and he rubbed his eyes sleepily. "What's going on? Why are you yelling?"

"Let's go. We've got work to do," said Aaduth importantly.

"It's too early," groaned Basadict, stepping all the way out and letting the stiff caribou skin slap back into place as he stretched his arms in the air and yawned widely.

"No, it's not. Look, the sun has moved above the trees," said Aaduth pointing in the direction of the surrounding hills that pushed up against the other side of the lake.

Basadict glanced in the direction and shrugged his shoulders in resignation.

Although he was only a year older than Basadict, Aaduth stood head and shoulders over his friend. Because of this, little Basadict deferred all decisions to Aaduth and tended to follow him without question.

Jaywritt watched them trudge across the clearing and disappear into the woods. He smiled and shook his head at their carefree approach to life. Luckily, neither of them had yet experienced the inevitable encounter with the Buggishaman. Since Shanadee's death, they had all stayed hidden in the forest, avoiding contact as much as they possibly could.

Every year there were more and more Buggishaman. They continued to move up the Great River and build their houses wherever they liked; fishing and hunting where his people had once been the only hunters. There was no way to stop it now. It would be like putting your hands in the Great River and expecting to push it back.

As he sat there, the faces of the rest of the tribe began to drift across his mind. Old Jeddilledt and his wife, Laddiwett, were the oldest; both in their fifties. That was old for a Beothuk, thought Jaywritt; not a lot of Beothuk got to live that long. They lived in the mamateek directly across from where he was sitting. Their daughter, Middadewann, lived with them along with her two children, Basadict and sweet little five-year-old Ebanthou. Middadewann's husband had been shot about four years ago by the Buggishaman, not too long after Ebanthou was born. He was probably one of the last Indians to be shot by the Buggishaman. He had been out at the coast with Laddiwett's brother, Tedashuit. They had been collecting shellfish in the shallow water when two Buggishaman ran out of the woods and started shooting. Tedashuit ran but Middadewann's husband died instantly. Before reaching the safety of the woods, Tedashuit was hit in the lower arm by the gunfire. He survived but his arm didn't.

Including Tedashuit, there were six in that mamateek.

In the smaller mamateek next to Jeddilledt's there were only four of the tribe. Langnon, Jeddilledt's son, lived there with his wife Godabonyee, their seven-year-old son Jiggameel, and Godabonyee's sister Hanawadet.

Jaywritt's mamateek held five people; his wife Doodlebewshet, their two children Aaduth and Linguitt, and his niece Shanawdithit, his sister Shanadee's daughter.

As the last of the faces slowly slipped across his mind, he felt himself shiver again because he knew there was nothing he could do now to change their fate. With their numbers down to fifteen, their future was undoubtedly sealed. It felt like Death had slipped his icy fingers down the back of his cloak to remind him that he was close by and waiting.

The carefree shouts of the two boys returning with firewood shook him out of his dark mood. They have no idea, he thought, wouldn't it be great to be like them.

His heart warmed and the tension melted out of his face as he listened to their light-hearted banter.

"I will bring you back the tooth of the first monau I kill," boasted Aaduth confidently.

"You have never seen a monau. How will you kill it?" taunted Basadict.

"I will spear it. You will see. Then we will see who gets to laugh."

"Maybe the monau will catch you, my friend," laughed Basadict.

"I will still take his tooth," said Aaduth with a grin as he gave Basadict a punch on the shoulder with his free hand.

Jaywritt leaned over, gripped the corner of the washawet skin, and pulled it back so the two boys could enter the mamateek. Doodlebewshet and Shanawdithit were kneeling on the ground rolling up their bed furs. The boys walked by them and dropped their loads of dry sticks near the fire pit, kicking up a small cloud of ash. Linguitt still lay wrapped in her furs. She had not been well lately. Jaywritt worried that she might have the Buggishaman's coughing sickness; she seemed to have all the signs.

The boys busied themselves, snapping the dead tree limbs into smaller pieces to get the fire started. Doodlebewshet rooted around the ashes with a stick until she uncovered some live embers. She cupped her hands around them and blew until they began to glow. Then she touched a piece of birch rind to the embers and immediately the flames flashed to life. Stacking the dry sticks that the boys were breaking up, she soon had the fire cracking and dancing merrily. The dark smoke that swirled toward the opening in the roof of the mamateek wrapped itself around the chill of the early morning air and dragged it along with it.

Jaywritt followed the boys into the mamateek and stacked the sharpened spears on an overhead rack. Reaching in behind them, he lifted out his long hathemay.

"I'm going hunting," he announced.

Standing in the dim light, he noticed the deep worry lines on his wife's face as she glanced toward the sleeping figure of their daughter.

"She'll be alright," he muttered softly to Doodlebewshet.

"I'm not sure she will," she replied. "She is getting worse every day. Nothing I do seems to help. I'm scared Jaywritt."

"I will take the boys and we will get some fresh meat. You can make her some stew. That should perk her up."

The two boys, who had overheard this conversation, scrambled to get Aaduth's hathemay and arrows, grinning widely as they rushed out the door.

Jaywritt followed them outside and watched as they disappeared through the door of Jeddilledt's mamateek, only to reappear in seconds with Basadict's hathemay and arrows.

Hearing all the commotion, Langnon pushed aside the skin door to his mamateek and peered outside.

"We're going hunting," said Jaywritt. "Are you coming?"

Langnon nodded and ducked back inside to get his hathemay.

With Jaywritt in the lead and Langnon at the rear, they set out following the river upstream. The sun had disappeared behind a large bank of clouds and the wind was trying its best to push the cold through their fur lined cloaks. Their breath was sending swirling clouds around their heads as they walked quickly out of sight of the mamateeks.

Not far out of camp Jaywritt stopped in the path and pointed to the tracks along the side of the trail. "See there, boys. Two caribou crossed the river here."

"Will we follow them, Father?"

"Yes," said Jaywritt over his shoulder as he broke into a run following the tracks away from the river. "No more talking."

They were moving through a stand of tall leafless birch. Ragged pieces of rind hung from the pale trunks, flapping noiselessly in the wind. The caribou trail zigzagged around the trees, seemingly in no particular direction. The boys were struggling to keep up with their leader and were slowly falling behind as the trail began to gently slope upwards, winding around the side of a small hill. Ahead of them, Aaduth saw his father drop to his knees and hold up his hand for quiet.

Breathing heavily, the boys scrambled up the slope and dropped to the ground behind Jaywritt. "What is it, Father?" gasped Aaduth.

Jaywritt pointed to the smaller footprints that intersected the caribou tracks just ahead. "Moisamadrook (wolves)," he whispered. "About five of them."

Aaduth glanced at Basadict. He could see his fear reflected in his friend's eyes. "Should we go back?" asked Basadict with a slight tremble in his voice.

Aaduth looked anxiously at his father. He was not excited about following a pack of moisamadrook, and he hoped his father wasn't either.

Looking over their heads at Langnon, Jaywritt quietly said, "I think we will follow them. They will only take one of the caribou." Much to the boy's dismay, Langnon nodded assent.

"Do you see anything?" whispered Aaduth.

"No," replied Basadict without pulling his eyes away from the shadowy woods around them, scanning them for signs of the hunters.

To the boys, Jaywritt said, "Keep an arrow in your hathemay and be ready. They probably already know we are here."

Nervously, the two boys pulled an arrow from their quivers and notched it in their hathemays. The men did the same.

Pushing to his feet, Jaywritt turned to follow the tracks, when suddenly the air was filled with a chorus of howls that made the hair leap erect on the boys' arms.

"It's OK," said Langnon, as he placed a steadying hand on Basadict's arm. "They have found the two caribou."

Swallowing loudly, Basadict scrambled to his feet and moved closer to his friend. The hathemay trembled in his hand. He kept turning, trying to see in all directions at once.

"Let's go," ordered Jaywritt as he began following the tracks again. "Quietly," he instructed over his shoulder as he moved out in a crouch, his hathemay at the ready.

They had only gone a short distance when the trail led them to a small clearing, visible ahead through the trees. Sleek gray figures were racing around the treeline, circling the two terrified animals in the centre. Great puffs of steam exploded from the nostrils of the two trapped animals as they snorted and pawed the ground. Their huge eyes were wide with fear, desperately searching for some way to escape.

The four moisamadrook had spaced themselves, as they continued to run the circle of trampled snow, two running in one direction and two in the other, waiting for one of the frightened caribou to break and run.

A large black male sat on his haunches at the edge of the clearing as if directing the hunt, occasionally throwing back his head and splitting the air with a blood curdling howl that struck fear in the onlookers and caribou alike. Each time, one of the runners would charge toward the caribou and stop short. The buck would drop its heavily antlered head, shaking it menacingly in the face of the moisamadrook until it backed away and joined the circle again. This tactic was repeated again and again, each time, a different moisamadrook would take the role of the aggressor.

The black male slowly and deliberately swung his head and looked over his shoulder in the direction of the watching Beothuk. Putting a steadying hand on the boys' shoulders, Jaywritt murmured, "Don't move."

Aaduth felt as if the cold black eyes had locked onto him and he shuddered in apprehension. He could feel the smoldering anger in their dark depths and he was glad he wasn't out here alone. He could feel Basadict shaking next to him.

The male turned back to the hunt, threw its head in the air, and released another spine-chilling howl. This time the frightened doe broke and ran toward the woods. No longer protected by the threatening antlers of the buck, she had given the moisamadrook the opening they were looking for. The pack was instantly on her, lunging and nipping at her heels, turning her back from the protection of the woods so that she was running within the trampled circle of the clearing. The black male stood to his feet and, with a low growl, charged at the exhausted doe, springing at her throat and pulling her off her feet. Joined by the savage pack, it was over in minutes and the doe lay in a crimson patch of snow, no longer moving.

The buck had escaped into the woods, running back the way they had come. As he raced by, Jaywritt had hit him with an arrow, high in the front shoulder.

Slowly the group backed away from the clearing and the frenzied feast that was taking place in front of them. Once Jaywritt thought they were far enough away, he turned and led them at a run, following the telltale spots of blood in the trail. Soon they came upon the wounded animal standing amongst the birch with its head bowed down to the ground, sucking great gasps of air into its tortured lungs. Jaywritt and Langnon's arrows brought it down.

Hurriedly they cleaned and carved the meat, keeping a close watch on the woods around them as they worked. No one spoke. As soon as the meat was divided up in manageable loads they headed back on the trail towards the river.

It was almost dark when they walked into camp.

Chapter 2
1823

A week had slipped by since the unforgettable encounter with the moisamadrook. It was an event that undoubtedly would never fade from the boys' memory as the scariest time of their lives, yet each day their story had grown some. The details continued to be embellished as time passed. Listening to them retell the adventure, it was a wonder they had all escaped with their lives, thought Jaywritt.

Today he and Aaduth would be leaving for the coast to hunt monau. It would take them three or four days to get there, so they would be gone from the camp for at least a couple of weeks. Lying in the dark, listening to the sounds of his family sleeping, he worried if everything would be ok while he was gone. Linguitt was getting worse. It was easy to see; her constant cough and fever left no doubt. She cried a lot now. She was not a strong girl, she never had been; and now with this sickness she had no will to do anything but lay on her bed all day. But he had to leave his worry in the hands of Doodlebewshet and Shanawdithit. They knew much better than he how to take care of her; nevertheless, he feared for her, and he couldn't help but wonder if she would be here when they got back.

From the still form lying next to him came a soft whisper. "It will be OK my husband. We will be fine."

He had thought he was the only one awake. Reaching his arm around her, he pulled her close to him underneath the old ragged washawet skin. The familiar smell of the monau oil in her long black hair filled his nostrils as he buried his face and sighed contentedly. "You have given me a good life, Doodlebewshet," he murmured then kissed her on the cheek. He sensed she was smiling at him in the dark as she slipped her hand into his and squeezed.

"I will start the fire," she said as she pushed the washawet skin away and stood to her feet.

Jaywritt rolled out of bed and stretched expansively. Through the silver streaks of dim light filtering down from the smoke hole in the roof, he could see Aaduth sitting up in his bed on the other side of the fire pit. He had slept with his hathemay and aaduth next to him. Although he had tried his best to hide it, his excitement had been written all over his face last night. Jaywritt wondered if he had slept at all. Smiling at him he said, "This is the big day, son."

Immediately Aaduth was on his feet. "I'm ready, Father."

It seemed he had abandoned his attempts to hide his excitement.

"OK Son, it won't be long now," laughed Jaywritt. "We'll have something to eat first."

The wigwam was slowly coming alive around him. The fire Doodlebewshet had coaxed to life from the embers buried in last night's ashes began to glow and flicker. The newly birthed flames licked hungrily at the dry sticks. The crack and pop of the burning sticks and the woody smell of smoke gave the room a sudden sense of warmth and feeling of home. This peaceful scene almost made him forget the troubles and bleak future of the tribe. It seemed like this life could go on forever. Perhaps it could.

Jaywritt watched Doodlebewshet pour a mixture of dried eggs and berries into the pot of simmering water. She is a good wife, he thought affectionately as he sat there watching her slowly stir the paste until it thickened. There was something calming about her slow deliberate movements. She had that way about her. Whenever he felt anxiety creeping up on him, he had always been able to lean on her. Her quiet strength had always helped quell the churning storm inside him.

Right now, the inside of Jaywritt's mouth was filling with saliva as the deliciously familiar aroma swirled through the air around him. He took the bowl of hot paste that Doodlebewshet held out to him and held it close to his nose.

"That smells good, Woman," he smiled.

Dipping his fingers in the mixture, he touched the hot liquid to his lips. "Mmm…it tastes even better than it smells!" he said with delight.

Jaywritt saw the smile of appreciation flicker across her face as she turned back to the pot and poured some out for their son.

The first night they camped near the constantly moving water of the Great River. In the distance they could hear the sound of the river tumbling over the falls. It was a quiet evening, the silence occasionally broken by the flittering songbirds in the trees above them and the crackling of the cooking fire. The sound of the falls stirred memories in Jaywritt that he was compelled to share with his son.

"I remember this place."

Aaduth lay back on the ground and locked his hands together behind his head. He liked to listen to his father's stories, and out here he had him all to himself. He smiled contentedly and stared up at the star-filled sky. This was starting out to be a good trip. He wished Basadict were here.

"I was only five. My sister Shanadee was fifteen. It was two years after the Buggishaman raided our camp and killed our mother and our brother Timmwall. Those who had escaped the raid decided to move back to the Great Lake to find other members of the tribe. They thought it would be safer there, away from the coast, and it would be easier to gather food with a larger group."

"It was a beautiful place Aaduth. I would like to take you there someday. I have some great memories of that place," he said as he tossed more sticks on the crackling fire.

"I would love to see the Great Lake, Father," Aaduth responded eagerly.

"Maybe next year after the snow melts. Anyway, we had travelled for three days before we reached the falls; the same ones you can hear now in the distance. Two tapaithooks (canoes) had been loaded down with our winter supply of meat and four of the older boys and girls were pulling them up the river. We camped at the top of the falls that night, not far from this very spot. The next day, we packed up everything and got ready to continue the trip. Before those of us who were walking left camp, we watched the tapaithooks as they were floated upriver. The girl who was steadying the second tapaithook lost her footing and, when she grabbed on to the boat to break her fall, she yanked the rope free from the boy who was holding it upriver. The swift current quickly swept her and the tapaithook downstream and over the falls. Later they found her body washed up on the shore farther downstream. Her name was Serondius. She is buried near here."

"That is a sad story, Father."

"Yes, Son. More than thirty winters have passed since that day and many things have happened to our tribe, but it still makes me sad to remember. It was a terrible day."

Jaywritt sat in silence for a while, idly poking at the fire with a stick. "I wish you could have known your aunt Shanadee," he said thoughtfully.

"Me too. I love your stories about her."

"She was a wonderful sister, strong and caring. She taught me many things about life. I wish I could show you where she rests, but the Buggishaman made sure that could never happen," he said angrily. "We never found her after they killed her."

"Your grandfather was named Nanolute," he continued. "Your grandmother's name was Manddilleeitt. You had one aunt named Shanadee and one uncle named Timmwall. I tell you this so you can remember."

"I know, Father. I remember. Someday I will tell my own son, and he will tell his son. Our story will not be forgotten."

"That is how we have always kept our story alive," said Jaywritt softly. Inside he was questioning whether there would come a day when no one was left to ensure their stories survived.

Chapter 3
1821

He was born in the dead of winter, somewhere in the high Arctic wasteland of snow and ice, with only the unrelenting howl of the bitter north wind to herald his arrival. He ate and slept beneath the frozen surface, with the hypnotic rhythm of his mother's heartbeat his only comfort. For the first few weeks he never left his mother's side.

After what seemed like an unending hibernation, his stomach was rumbling for more than just his mother's milk. Just like all bear cubs, he craved meat. It had been a long winter, but now he was finally clawing his way out of the frozen cave. He and his twin sister emerged from the tunnel of snow and were thrust into a vast sea of dazzling, endless white.

His sister seemed to be as taken with this new landscape as he was. At first she just stood there on wobbly legs, staring in amazement at the ice and snow; it went on forever. There was so much more space to play in. Running awkwardly on her rubber legs, that until now she had only slept on, she charged at him and bowled him over in the snow. Being a little bigger, she had the advantage and managed to knock him down. She continued this game each time he made it back on his feet.

In frustration, he nipped at her ears, maybe a little harder than he should have, but it didn't seem to dampen her enthusiasm in the least. She took it as a sign that he was finally getting into the game, which quickly turned into a wrestling match. She knew she could take him. This was going to be fun.

Suddenly, she heard a low rumbling growl. It was her mother. It was enough to interrupt the game and allow her brother to scramble to his feet and race across the frozen surface. Having reached what he felt was a safe distance, at the base of a large mound of snow, he immediately turned and taunted her.

Without hesitation, she launched herself across the gap he had opened between them. This time he was ready. He turned and raced up the incline, making sure he didn't get too far ahead. The snow leveled out at the top and she began to gain on him. For a brief moment he was afraid his plan wasn't going to work and he pushed himself to stay ahead of her. Finally, he skidded to a stop, turned, and flopped on his belly as if giving up, but at the last minute he rolled out of the way. He watched with delight as the momentum of her victory charge carried her over the edge and out of sight. He jumped to his feet and peered over the peak just in time to see her go tumbling down the other side. By the time she reached the bottom she was twice as big as she had been at the top, tightly wrapped in a ball of snow.

It was the funniest thing he had ever seen. He grinned triumphantly down at her as she struggled to her feet and kicked away her new coat of snow. She glanced up at him in disgust, turned her back, and strutted off in the direction of their mother.

Standing there, at the top of the world, he felt good. He had beaten her and he knew this would not be the last time. He slowly turned full circle, surveying the canvas of white. Lifting his nose in the air, he caught the faint scent of something salty being carried across the ice on the cold, crisp wind. It was a new, strange scent that triggered a memory buried deep inside; something that had been placed there at birth. He felt drawn to follow it. He turned toward where his mother and sister had been. They were already some distance away, padding across the ice in the direction he felt he needed to go. He slid down off the mound on his stomach and followed them.

As he walked behind them, he noticed the scent was growing stronger and he quickened his step. Before long, he could see darker patches ahead in the otherwise unbroken white. His mother led them up to one of the larger patches and with a splash, disappeared into the dark. He looked at his sister questioningly, not sure what to do next. Suddenly, his mother's head appeared again. She shook, spraying them with droplets of the dark water. Without realizing, he licked some of the salty water from his face. It was the smell that had drawn him here. With a squeal of delight, he leapt into the water next to his mother. Seconds later, he surfaced, coughing and spitting out water, but still happily paddling around in circles.

His sister still stood on the ice looking on, with no intention of venturing in. He watched as his mother hooked her giant claws into the ice and drew herself out of the water near where his sister stood. Without warning, she placed her nose behind her reluctant cub and nudged. To his glee, his sister lost her footing, went sliding across the wet surface, and plopped into the water.

When she reappeared, he was there. He placed his feet on her shoulders and pushed her under again.

A low growl interrupted their play and he turned to see his mother moving away across the ice. His stomach rumbled as he pulled himself out of the water. He had forgotten how hungry he was. Quickening his pace, he loped after her.

They encountered more and more patches of water and the land became more uneven, with higher hills and sharp jutting pieces of ice that littered the landscape.

In the distance, he could see dark spots on the ice near some of the water holes. Some of them moved occasionally. A new scent drifted across his nose, making his mouth water and his stomach answer in anticipation. Instinctively, he knew this was food.

With a warning grunt, his mother signalled them to stay and she slowly pushed herself across the surface on her belly until she was lying near a small hole in the ice. She lay there unmoving until something slipped out of the water onto the ice near her.

She delivered lunch to them where they lay. His first taste of the fresh meat awakened a new hunger in him and he knew he would never go back to the milk diet he had only known until now.

He was a very quick learner and his body soon craved more of the tasty meat. Later that week found him camped out near a hole in the ice, quietly watching and waiting. It wasn't long before a head popped out of the water and scanned the surrounding ice. Like his mother, he didn't move a muscle as he watched the seal check for danger. Without moving his head, he glanced over at his sister who had fallen asleep near where his mother was laying on the ice. Well, there will be no meat for her, he thought.

The seal took one last look and ducked under the water. Thanks to his white coat, he had gone undetected on the snowy ice. With a splash, the seal shot out of the hole on-to the ice, followed by three more of its kind in quick succession. He met his mother's eyes. They told him to wait. The seals had grown more comfortable with their surroundings and moved farther away from the hole to find the best spot in the sun. He saw his mother's front legs tense and he knew it was time. Together, they rushed across the ice at the startled animals and he took his first seal. Standing over his kill, he looked triumphantly at his sister who finally had awakened and was standing there looking confused.

With his change in diet came a sudden growth spurt and he soon surpassed his sister in weight. This signalled the end of her reign of terror over him. For nearly two years he bullied his sister, taking what he wanted, when he wanted it. He was smart enough to stay away from his mother's giant swinging paws, most of the time. She was only fast enough to club him twice for stealing his sister's food. He sometimes wondered if his mother intentionally missed. He thought she probably did.

Realization that he need not fear any other animal was soon to come, and when he struck out on his own on his second birthday he did so with attitude. He was master of his kingdom and he needed no one but himself; not his mother, and especially not his sister. He intended to explore every inch of what he considered his territory.

Wandering aimlessly around the densely packed ice field, one day he found a large ice pan. Above the water, it resembled a small rugged island. Below the water, it was a massive ice structure with shelves and caves carved over decades of time as it had been slowly birthed in the far north. It had somehow broken free and was slowly making its inevitable journey south, where, in time, it would transform itself into the very water that now carried it along. The currents barely moved the massive iceberg as it lumbered along the Labrador coast, sometimes scraping the ocean bottom in the darkness far below.

A natural cave, high in one of the peaks, gave him an unobstructed view. From there he could spot the seals sunning themselves on the flat ice pans that slowly drifted through the water with them. He was content to ride the ice flow south, feasting on seals as he drifted along. He had no companions. He was alone and he liked it that way. Day after day, he ate his fill and slept in the ice cave. No one bothered him. Life was good.

The ice flow slowly moved along the rugged and barren coastline. Days turned to weeks. Time for him was measured in darkness and light. He hunted and ate to no set schedule. When his hunger became strong he left his cave and found food, otherwise, he slept or contentedly watched the slowly changing scenery from the high perch on his ice island.

Lately, he noticed the water was getting warmer and the ice was thinning out. Most of the flat ice had disappeared, leaving only the larger bergs, like his, and even they floated farther and farther apart. The seals were no longer as plentiful; they seemed to have disappeared along with the flat ice.

Much of his time these days was spent sleeping. But now the rumbling in his stomach disturbed his sleep, reminding him that he had not eaten today. This might be his last day on the berg. He had already decided he would not go much farther. It was no longer comfortable and he realized the time had come to abandon his temporary home and return to the cold snow covered land he had left behind. He was reminded of his mother.

He remembered how she had taught him to hunt. He wondered how she was. He even missed his pesky sister, as he thought back to their playtimes, all while slowly drifting back to sleep. But then something interrupted his nap. A sound. It was an unusual sound, a new sound, one he had not heard before. From where he lay, he raised his head and peered out the open mouth of the ice cave. He sniffed the air, trying to identify the source, but could not detect anything new. Silver droplets dripped from the top of the cave opening, where the sun was turning the century old ice into water. The harsh glare bouncing off the wet surface burned his eyes. Squinting sleepily, he scanned the open water around him trying to locate the source of the sound.

Movement on an ice pan close to the shoreline caught his eye. There he saw two strange animals. These were animals he had not encountered before. They seemed only to move on two legs. Something stirred deep in his memory. It seemed to be warning him of some danger, but he couldn't seem to piece it together.

He watched with interest as the larger one used a long stick to pull a seal up onto the ice pan where they were standing. Watching it wiggle and flounder on the ice, he was suddenly reminded of his fierce hunger. That was his seal. He had to have it. He must have it. Sliding noiselessly down the wet slippery slope, he slipped into the icy water, barely making a ripple.

With powerful strokes, he swiftly closed the distance between them, and when he reached the ice where he had seen the strange animals, he slipped his head above the surface. The scent of fresh blood slammed into his probing nostrils, removing any thought of caution that may have lurked below the surface of his mind. His need for food, and its close proximity, took complete control and pushed all other thoughts away. With a powerful kick of his hind legs, he pushed out of the water onto the same ice pan were the two-legged animals stood. He focused in on the larger of them, the one who was bent over the bleeding seal; his seal. His tongue whipped across his lips, tasting the scent. He crouched low, storing his strength in his paws, and with one firm push, he lunged.

Chapter 4
1823

The coastline was littered with drift ice, just as it always was this time of year. Most of it was nuzzled up against the beach as if trying to escape its inevitable demise as it journeyed south into warmer waters. Some of the luckier ones were stranded on the beaches, left behind by the retreating tide. They had already come too far south to survive, but at least here on the shore they would get to live a little longer.

As he rowed his small boat along the edge of the gently rocking ice field, Andrew had time to think. Sarah's words were bothering him. He'd always known her desire to have a child was a lot stronger than she had ever let on. Over the past twelve years since they had been together he had been unable to fulfil that need for her. Although she never said anything to him about it, he blamed himself for their inability to complete their family. She had been restless and talked in her sleep again last night. It had awoken him just before dawn when he heard her straining to cry out to their son, a son they never had. He knew it wasn't just a dream. It was something that was on her mind before she fell asleep. It was something that he felt was always on her mind. It was important to her; he knew that with a certainty.

He often wondered if she was happy here on this isolated island, so far away from home. Home, where she had been surrounded by a large family, was now a world away. It was a world they would probably never see again, family that was lost to them. Here in this new land they seldom saw anyone. It was a lonely and desolate place but they had carved out a piece for themselves. They had made a new home in the little cove on the other side of the point. He thought she was happy, well, apart from the lack of children. He had done everything he could to make her life good. She was the best thing that had ever happened to him. He would never have survived out here without her.

They had quickly learned this new land demanded a heavy toll before surrendering up a living. The climate was harsh and unforgiving. The soil was rocky and thin. It had been much worse than they had expected when they arrived but they were both determined to make it work, and together they had.

He expected the harder years were behind them now. They built a comfortable house and set a large vegetable garden. Fishing was good and game was plentiful. They would never want for something to eat.

Through it all Sarah had been at his side, doing whatever needed to be done to clear the land and build their house. She was a hard worker and pushed him through the hard times when he wondered if there really was any future here for them at all. He knew in a lot of ways she was stronger than him and her determination had gotten them to where they were now. He wished he could give her the child that he knew she so desperately wanted. If truth were known, he wouldn't mind a little one running around either.

Looking back over the stern of the punt, he could see a thin vein of smoke rising above the top of the tree line. A smile lifted the corners of his mouth. She was there, probably standing over the old iron stove busily cooking their evening meal. In his mind's eye he could picture her. She was wearing the dark navy dress with a full length apron covering the front. Her dark red hair would be wound up into a bun at the back, held in place with the long silver pin he had bought her last year from the trader out of St. John's. A dusting of flour would have found its way into her hair as it always did when she was baking. Dark stains from blueberries and raspberries were permanently blended into the once white apron where she wiped her hands. He could almost hear her singing as she bustled around the kitchen and pantry. She always sang or hummed when she worked. It made the little one room cabin feel warm and cozy. Those were times he loved, when they were together like that, late in the evening after his day's work was done.

He shouldn't go much farther. He didn't want to be late; but he still hadn't gotten a seal. That was why he was out here in the first place. This was the best time of year to catch seals as they followed the drift ice as it moved south along the coast. Resting the end of the paddles on his knees, he glanced over his shoulder to check how close he was to the large iceberg that had grounded on the point just ahead of him. It towered over him like a large white mountain. The glare of the sun bouncing off the smooth glassy surface blinded him, forcing him to release one of the paddles so he could shade his eyes with his hand.

"I wonder how far that one travelled?" he said aloud. "Must be some old. Bet there's stuff frozen inside from hundreds of years ago. I'd say it's got lots a stories to tell."

He held the paddles above the water and let the boat drift toward the giant berg as he sat there studying the mountain of ice, imagining where it had been.

Craning his neck back, he could see what looked like a shallow cave near the top of one of the peaks.

"Wonder if some animal might have used that for a home when it was up north? Be able to see a long way from up there."

Long before he reached the side of the berg he could see it stretching out underneath the boat.

"This thing is massive. Guess I shouldn't get too close. Don't want something breaking off and swampin' me boat," he muttered.

Dipping the paddles back into the water, he swung the boat away from the iceberg and slowly rowed around the end of it, watching for signs of life as it passed behind him. I still got to get that seal and it's getting late, he thought. Sarah will be expecting me soon.

Suddenly his thoughts were interrupted by a commotion near the beach. He turned on his seat in time to see a large polar bear towering over the prostrate figure of what looked to be a Beothuk Indian on a flat ice pan. Near the figure, with his back to Andrew, was a terrified young boy. He was on one knee with a drawn bow, yelling at the top of his lungs at the giant bear.

The polar bear stood with its massive paw on the chest of the fallen Beothuk while tearing at the flesh of the seal that was impaled on the Indian's spear. It swung its head and looked menacingly at the boy as it devoured the bloody meat, a low threatening rumble rattled from its blood smeared maw.

"Hey," Andrew yelled, trying to distract the huge beast, as he swung his paddles aboard. He felt his stomach tighten into knots as he lifted his long gun from the bottom of the gently rocking boat and pushed to his feet. He spread his feet wide apart in an effort to brace himself. He was close enough to take the shot. He hoped the boat would be steady enough, as he looked down the length of the barrel at the huge target.

"Git down," he shouted, frantically motioning to the boy to lay flat on the ice. Either the boy didn't hear him or he was frozen with terror, because he continued to kneel facing the bear, directly in line between Andrew and the huge animal. It was a long shot, and there was a chance he would hit the boy, but he knew he had to take it or the bear would get the young Beothuk anyway.

Aaduth watched his father thrust his aaduth into the second monau and pull it up on the ice. Glancing over his shoulder, he squinted, as he peered almost directly into the sun. He could just make out the dark smudge where the first one was lying on an ice pan closer to shore. They had surprised it while it was sunning itself on the beach. Afterward, they made their way across the pieces of floating ice to the edge of the flow. That was a scary and exciting run, jumping from one rocking ice pan to the next. Sometimes there was room for both of them, but some of the pans were only big enough for one at a time. He had narrowly avoided falling into the water several times, and out here at the edge of the ice the water was a lot deeper. It made him a little nervous. He turned back to watch his father.

It was time he killed a monau of his own. He needed a story to tell Basadict. Three monau had slipped into the water from the pan when he and his father had jumped onto it. One was squirming on the end of his father's aaduth so there were two more in the water somewhere.

He was reaching for his aaduth lying near his feet when the ice suddenly lurched and he stumbled backward. Looking over his shoulder as he was falling, he gasped in surprise as he saw a huge white monster break through the surface of the water. It dug its long curved claws into the frozen surface and pulled itself onto their ice pan. He had never seen an animal this big. It was massive. Pools of water poured from its thick white fur coat, collecting on the ice where it stood. Aaduth was scared. He tried to yell a warning but no sound came from his dry throat. With a speed that would have matched a much leaner animal, it lunged across the ice and leapt on his father, pinning him to the ice. The loud crack that he heard when his father hit the ice frightened him. Aaduth was sure he heard bones breaking, and it definitely wasn't the monster's. He pulled himself to his knees. The white surface of the ice was turning red around his father. Blood was dripping from gashes in his coat and a stain was spreading out from in under his head. He was not moving.

Without thinking, Aaduth slipped his hathemay from his shoulder and notched an arrow. He knew he had no chance of winning this fight but the beast was killing his father; he must try. Pulling back the string as far as he could manage, he sighted along the trembling arrow at the monster's throat. He found his voice and yelled at the top of his lungs to get the animal's attention. It turned toward him. He let out his breath and released the string. Suddenly, he heard a shout. Whipping his head around, he saw a small boat and a Buggishaman with a gun pointed in his direction. But the deafening roar of the monster caught his full attention and he turned back to see it flailing its head from side to side in a rage. The arrow had found its mark and was sticking out of its neck. He didn't know which would get him first, the great beast or the Buggishaman behind him. The bitter taste of fear filled his mouth as his trembling hands notched a second arrow and he stared into the dark enraged eyes of the monster. Red froth flicked from its gaping mouth as it flung its head back and roared again. Lifting the hathemay, he pulled the string taut for what he knew would be his last shot. But before he could loose his arrow, there was an explosion. The monster's head suddenly jerked and blood spurted from an opening near its ear. The explosion he heard had been the sound of a gunshot. The monster tumbled to the ice as Aaduth swung around on his knee, pointing the arrow at the Buggishaman.

Andrew shook his head in disbelief at what he had just seen. The young Beothuk boy had stood his ground and shot an arrow into the polar bear. He couldn't be any more than 9 or 10 years old. He had never seen such bravery. I can't wait to tell Sarah about this one, he thought.

The boat's momentum had brought him closer to the large ice pan. He knew he had to try and shoot the bear. It was the only chance the boy had. It wasn't going to be an easy shot. Shooting from a boat was never easy, although the water was fairly calm as he drifted closer to the ice. To make things worse, the boy was directly between him and the bear. He pressed the stock of his gun firmly against his shoulder and sighted down the long barrel. The bear was thrashing its head back and forth, roaring wildly. It had now turned its attention to the young Indian and Andrew saw the great muscles of its hind legs bunch as it prepared to charge the kneeling boy. It was as if time had slowed. Staring down the barrel, it seemed the tiny bead at the end was so insignificant against the bulk of the angry bear. He felt little drops of cold sweat trickle down his forehead as he tried to steady his hands. The head of the bear filled his vision and he increased the pressure on the trigger. He took a deep breath and held it. Then he dropped the barrel a little to compensate for the kick of the gun, and squeezed. The explosion knocked him back and he almost lost his footing, but he saw with satisfaction the bear's head jerk with the impact. He watched it stumble to the side and collapse on top of the Indian man lying on the ice. The smell of burnt gun powder slowly drifted back over him.

"Now that's a good shot," he said grinning with pleasure, and a little more than a touch of relief.

But to his surprise, the boy had swung around on his knee and was now taking aim at him.

"Hey Boy, don't aim that thing at me. I'm not here to hurt you," he said calmly.

Andrew slowly lowered the gun and placed it on the floor of the boat. He raised his hands to show the boy they were empty, picked up one of the paddles, and maneuvered the boat to the ice pan.

Aaduth knelt there, staring down the length of the arrow at the Buggishaman. He could feel the cold from the ice seeping through the knee of his leggings. The muscles of his arms and back were burning from the strain of holding the string taut. He was torn between releasing the arrow and running to help his father. And then there was the monster. Maybe it wasn't dead. The Buggishaman had shot it with his gun. Does he only want the animal or did he do it to protect me? he wondered. He had lowered his gun in the face of Aaduth's arrow. Was that a sign of peace? It must be. He had to help his father. He released the tension on the hathemay, turned his back on the Buggishaman, and cautiously approached the monster. It had fallen across his father and wasn't moving. It looked dead. With his arrow at the ready, he kicked at its bloody head. He looked the beast in its eye and there was no life in the darkness that stared back at him. Dropping the hathemay and arrow on the ice, he tried to lift the beast off his father. Digging his heels into the rough surface of the ice pan, he strained with all his might but the huge animal did not move. It was way too heavy.

He heard the boat bump lightly against the ice pan and the shuffle of feet approaching him from behind. The Buggishaman dropped to his knees on the ice, pushed his arms under the monster, and began to lift it. He was still talking.

Aaduth had never been this close to a Buggishaman. It was a little unnerving. He did not look at him, but strained to push the monster. With their combined effort, the animal finally began to move, and together they lifted and rolled the beast away from his father.

Aaduth sat on the blood stained ice and cradled his father's head in his lap. He knew his spirit had left and was already on the journey to Gosset to join the many that had gone on before. The tears began as a trickle, but quickly turned into a torrent. His body shook with great sobs as his grief flowed from him in a rushing river. After some time, he became aware of a hand resting on his heaving shoulder and, through watery eyes, saw the Buggishaman looming over him. In other times, he would have been terrified of the contact, but he somehow knew this one meant him no harm. The Buggishaman knelt on the ice next to him, wrapped his arm around his shoulders, and drew him close against his chest. He held him there until the sobs subsided.

Aaduth felt himself being gently lifted to his feet. He knew of the danger he was in. All his life he had been taught to avoid the Buggishaman. He had been told story after story of how the Buggishaman killed Beothuks. Most of his own family had been killed at their hand. So why was this one showing him kindness?

Was it some trick? He had no idea what to do. There was nowhere to run. Besides, he didn't want to leave his father.

Andrew left the boy and walked back to the boat. The boy's emotions had moved him deeply. He knew he had to help him. He couldn't abandon him here, alone like this. He wished Sarah were here, she would know what to do. She was better at this than he was.

His boat was rocking gently in the icy water at the end of the rope tied to the small anchor he had driven into the surface of the ice. He stooped, grasped the rope, and pulled the boat part way onto the surface. Returning to the two Beothuks, he said to the boy, "I'm going to take your father in the boat." Using signs as best he could, he indicated to the boy what he planned to do. The boy seemed to understand. Gently, he lifted the dead Beothuk's shoulders off the ice, slipped his arms around his chest, and stood to his feet. Slowly he backed toward the punt, dragging the tall man with him. When he reached the boat he tried his best to gently lift him into it, but the weight was too much and he had no choice but to heave him aboard. The boy gathered up their weapons and followed him. He jumped into the boat without Andrew having to ask and settled on the floor next to his father.

"I'll get the seal," said Andrew. "I've got to get the skin off that bear as well," he continued in his one sided conversation with the boy. He knew the Indian did not understand but he kept talking anyway. Maybe it was because he didn't often have anyone to talk to. It felt good to talk, and it was probably helping calm the boy.

Returning to the bear, he examined the carcass of the seal. It had been torn up and partially eaten, so he left it where it was. He had noticed the other one on the ice back near the point, so he set out across the floating pans to get it. Before dragging it back to the boat, he opened it with his knife and removed the insides. Then he hooked it with his gaff, made his way back, and tossed it into the back of the boat.

"That will make a fine supper, Son," he said. "Sarah will make a good stew with this one. She's one great cook." He smiled at the boy sitting on the floor and went back to skin the bear.

Skinning the bear took some time. As he worked he noticed the boy was watching him from the boat. When he was ready to pull the bear skin to the boat the boy jumped out and helped him.

"That's a good sign," muttered Andrew to himself. "I guess he's not afraid of me anymore. I wonder what is going through his mind. This must all be some scary for him."

Once they loaded the bear skin, they pushed the boat back into the water and got in. Andrew picked up the paddles, fit them in the oar locks, and began to row the boat back the way he had come. He watched the boy sitting there on the floor at the stern of the boat. He wondered where he had come from and what his story was. He figured the best thing was to keep talking to him; it might make him feel a little more at ease.

"I'm taking you home to meet Sarah. You probably have nowhere else to go anyway. They say around here that most of the Beothuks are gone now. You two might even be the last of them. You will like Sarah. She loves children. She's always saying how terrible it is that all the Indians are dyin' off."

Chapter 5
1823

Sarah smiled contentedly as she looked around the one-room house Andrew had built for them. It wasn't much but it was clean and always warm in the winter. Andrew had picked a good spot for it, just at the treeline and far enough back from the beach to keep it out of the wind. One of the two windows overlooked the sheltered harbour and provided an evening view of the sunset when the sky was clear. Their bed sat at one end of the house and the table at the other, with the stove between them. In the corner sat a firewood box next to a flour barrel, which was underneath several shelves where she kept her dishes. That was all they really needed for the two of them.

She had her vegetable garden out back to tend to and Andrew fished and hunted for their food. It wasn't a bad life at all. Might be fun to have a little one running around though. But it seems that isn't going to happen, she thought sadly. She gave a little sigh as she scooped a handful of flour and lightly sprinkled the worn top of the wooden table. She dropped the dough on the flour and began kneading it again. Glancing out the front window, she spotted the boat coming around the point. She swept the stray strands from her face with flour filled hands, making a few more white streaks in her dark red hair. Walking across the room to the window that faced the harbour, she squinted her eyes and peered at the boat in the distance. It seemed to be riding lower in the water and there was definitely more than one person in the boat. "Andrew Foss, what have you gotten yourself into this time?" she murmured aloud.

Turning back to the table, she dumped the kneaded dough into two iron pans and left it to rise. She would bake the bread on the stove later.

She brushed her hands together several times and then wiped what flour remained in the tail of her apron. Slipping her coat from the peg behind the door, she shoved her arms into the sleeves, stepped out the door, and hurried down the short path to the beach. As she navigated around the bigger rocks, she held her collar together with one hand to keep out the March evening chill.

They were close enough now for her to see the other person sitting on the floor at the stern of the boat. With surprise, she stopped in her tracks. It's a Beothuk boy. What's Andrew doing with him? she wondered.

Noticing the boy was intently watching something on the beach, Andrew glanced over his shoulder. Seeing Sarah on the path, he turned, waved, and shouted, "Hey Sarah, we've got company."

Aaduth watched the Emamoose (white woman) as she made her way down the rocky path from the house. Her stained white apron fluttered in the wind as she hurried along with her head down. She had hair like fire, the reddest he had ever seen. He had heard stories told around the campfire of red-haired Emamoose. Some said it was a special omen, that these women were protected by the Gods. He wondered about that. There hadn't been much protection for their tribe, so it probably wasn't true for the red-haired Emamoose either. He glanced up at the Emamoose, who had now stopped on the path, and he shifted restlessly. The ribs of the small boat were sticking in his back and would not allow him to get comfortable.

So much had happened this day, his mind couldn't take it all in. This was the day he had almost died. Maybe he should have. He had no idea what was in store for him now. His eyes were drawn to the crumpled figure of his father lying just behind the Buggishaman at the front of the boat. Tears trickled down his face as the events of the day swam through his head and he slumped against the side of the boat. After all that had happened he found himself no longer caring about his own fate.

He wondered how his sister and mother were back at the camp. They had been very sick when he and father had left for the coast. Father thought it was the Buggishaman's disease, and if it was then there was little hope for them. He had no idea how to get back there without Father. He had no way to help anyone.

His eyes came to rest on the monau and he remembered the promise he had made to Basadict. He determined to get one of the teeth when the Buggishaman carved it up for food. He would keep it with him until he saw his friend again.

Sarah waved to Andrew and started moving again. She met the boat as it pushed aside several of the small ice pans floating at the shoreline, ground into the small beach rock, and came to a stop. She grabbed the keel and steadied it as Andrew jumped over the side into the shallow water and helped drag it onto the beach. By now she could see the second Beothuk lying in the bottom of the boat next to the seal and large polar bear skin. Her mind was racing with questions. Turning to Andrew, she anxiously asked, "What happened here? Are you alright? Who *is* this?"

"I'm fine Sarah," he smiled. "I'll tell you all about it when we get to the house. I'm pretty sure that one there was his father. I have to help the boy bury him first."

"Oh my, Andrew, he must be so scared. Did you see it happen?"

"I did. It was the bear. But Sarah, he was the bravest boy I've ever seen. He stood up to the bear with that little bow even though he must have known he could never win. You should have seen him. He was something else!"

He watched as Sarah's eyes filled up and washed away any doubt of what he already knew he had to do.

"I think we should keep him here with us, if he'll stay," he blurted out.

Sarah's breath caught in her throat and her hand went to her mouth as she stared at Andrew in disbelief.

"Do you mean that, Andrew?"

Andrew smiled at her and just nodded.

"Do you think he'll stay?"

"I think he might. Especially after he gets a taste of your baking," he chuckled.

He enjoyed watching Sarah get flustered. It didn't happen often but it was always fun to watch when it did. He grinned at her confusion. He could just imagine all the things that were going through her mind right now. On the one hand, she was struggling to contain her excitement at the thought of having the boy around the house, and on the other, trying not to get her hopes up.

"I'll go back up to the house and get it ready," she finally said, and started back up the hill almost at a run.

Andrew turned back to the boat and pulled the seal and the bear skin out over the side. But he would need the boy's help with the other load. He grimly motioned to the boy as he placed his hands under the arms of the dead Beothuk man, and together they carefully lifted the boy's father out of the boat and onto the beach.

Chapter 6
1823

Laddiwett stood in the middle of the muddy clearing and watched as Doodlebewshet and the two girls slowly walked down the path and disappeared into the woods. She did not know what was going to happen to them but she knew she would never see them again. It had not been easy, telling them to go, but she knew it was necessary to protect the few of them that remained. It was not just her right but her duty as the oldest woman in the camp. It was obvious to her that Doodlebewshet's daughter, Linguitt, had the dreaded Buggishaman's coughing disease and, for all she knew, it may have already been too late. She probably should have told them to leave before now.

Turning to her husband Jeddilledt, she nodded, "Do what you must do."

Stepping inside their mamateek, he emerged a few moments later with a burning stick in his hand and walked across the clearing to Jaywritt and Doodlebewshet's mamateek.

He touched the fiery stick against the birch covering and the ravenous flame leapt up the side and quickly engulfed the tent, consuming everything inside that had been in contact with the disease.

The little group of ten stood there, sadly watching as the dark smoke spiraled up into the sky and slowly drifted away, carrying with it the last reminders of their friends.

Laddiwett coughed, spitting out the taste of the smoke that lingered in the air. There was nothing left but a pile of ash behind the boulder where Jaywritt always sat. She shuffled back across the clearing and pushed through the door of her mamateek.

She was still coughing as she went and sat by the smoldering fire in the centre.

"Are you alright?" asked Jeddilledt, as he let the door flap fall into place behind him. "We had no choice you know."

"Are you sure? There is not enough of us left to be sending people away," she muttered. "Probably makes no difference anyway."

"That might be true, but we have to try and protect those of us who are left, especially the children."

"There's ten of us Jeddilledt. What are the chances any of us will survive? Maybe we should just give up and die. I'm sure that would make the Buggishaman happier…to be finally rid of us all."

Jeddilledt noticed the glisten in his wife's eyes and the falter in her voice as she spoke. It tore at his heart. They had been together long enough for him to know how much she was hurting right now.

They had seen a lot of their friends die at the hand of the Buggishaman; some directly and some by the disease they had brought with them. Now three more of them were gone, and Jaywritt and Aaduth still had not returned from the coast.

"How did this disease get in our camp anyway? We haven't had any contact with the Buggishaman. I don't understand this," she said.

"I do, Mother," Middadewann said quietly.

Laddiwett looked up sharply at her daughter sitting on the other side of the fire. "What do you mean?"

"I know how this started."

"But how could you know that?"

"It was Linguitt."

"Linguitt?"

"Yes mother. I couldn't tell you until now."

"Why?"

"She had contact with a Buggishaman. A sick Buggishaman."

"Linguitt?"

"Yes. She had an encounter with a trapper."

"When?"

"It was several weeks ago. One day she was on the trail and was surprised by him. She ran, but he caught her and forced himself on her."

"How do you know this?"

"I found her on the trail. Her clothes were torn off and she was bleeding. At first she wouldn't tell me what happened. She was scared, but I finally coaxed it out of her. I promised I wouldn't tell anyone."

Laddiwett glanced at Jeddilledt who had been listening quietly.

"I knew Father would have to kill her. He is the oldest and he would have to honor our custom. I didn't want that for either of them. Now it doesn't matter anymore. She is gone."

"Yes she is," muttered Jeddilledt.

"So the Buggishaman was sick?" asked Laddiwett.

"Yes. Linguitt later told me he was coughing and spitting blood."

"Nothing we can do to change it now, but you may have killed us all," Laddiwett said bitterly.

Chapter 7
1823

"Where did you get that?" asked Basadict, indicating the garden prong lying on the ground in front of Tedashuit.

"From a Buggishaman's shack down-river."

Basadict placed the partially filled basket on the ground and picked up the prong. The wooden handle had splintered and broken off just above the rusted metal. The four thin pointed teeth were at least twice the length of his hand.

"These will make good spear points, Tedashuit," he said as he stabbed them into the ground.

Tedashuit smiled at the boy. He had watched him grow from a baby and he had been like a father to the boy since his own father had been killed on that fateful trip to the coast.

"I can see you were roaming the bogs today," he said as he stared down at the boy's mud covered moccasins.

"I was picking plants for Mother," Basadict replied as he found a dry place to sit across from Tedashuit.

"Not much out there yet. Most of the trees are only just starting to get their leaves. It'll be another couple of weeks before everything turns green again."

"I found most of what she was looking for. I also got some dried sap from the trees," grinned Basadict.

Tedashuit smiled at the boy. "You know how much I love to chew that stuff, don't you?"

"Try some," said Basadict, as he held out the basket of plants and dried sap.

Tedashuit reached out with his right hand but suddenly stopped in mid motion, realizing what he was doing. Being right-handed, he naturally favored that hand, but it wasn't there anymore. Only a stump remained where his hand had once been, serving as a constant reminder of that day at the coast; the day that Basadict's father had been shot and killed. He had been lucky enough to get away with only the loss of his hand; at least that's what the others said. He was not so sure there was anything lucky about it though. What good was a one-armed hunter anyway? He was more of a burden to the tribe than anything else.

Switching sides with a sheepish grin, he picked a piece of the dried sap from Basadict's basket, popped it into his mouth, and began to chew. He savoured the sharp tang of the first bites, as the brittle sap crumbled into tiny pieces in his mouth. But as he swirled those small crumbs around the inside of his mouth, they soon transformed into a gummy paste that would last most of the rest of the day. Grinning with satisfaction at Basadict, he took another piece. "Now you'd best take the plants into your mother so she can start cooking."

Basadict pushed himself to his feet and turned toward the mamateek across the clearing. Smoke drifted lazily into the late afternoon sky from the hole at the top of the tent. Inside, he could hear his mother singing as she prepared their evening meal. Over the song he heard old Jeddilledt coughing. They were all worried about that. They didn't share their concerns with him, they probably thought he was too young for such things, but he had seen the telltale glances amongst the adults whenever the coughing started.

Turning back to Tedashuit, he said, "Can I go with you next time?"

"Where?"

"Downriver."

"I guess so, if it is ok with your mother."

"I'll check with her."

Happily chewing the gummy sap, Tedashuit watched the boy as he hurried across the clearing and disappeared inside the mamateek. He picked up his hatchet and hammered the first tooth of the garden prong until it was bent all the way back on itself. Then he turned it over and hammered it back in the other direction. Pinning the prong under his knee, he grasped the tooth with his left hand and worked it back and forth until the rusty metal snapped off.

While he worked he debated whether or not he should take the boy with him. It should be alright if they were careful, he supposed. After all, he had never run into the Buggishaman on his trips before, and he loved Basadict's company. It was at least a two day trip each way so they would get to spend a lot of time together. That would be fun, and it would give him a chance to teach the boy some things about the woods.

It would be good to get him away from here for a while anyway. There were signs of the Buggishaman's coughing sickness in their mamateek. Getting him away now might save him, maybe both of them.

He didn't expect a good outcome for his sister Laddiwett and her husband Jeddilledt. The coughing had gotten worse lately.

His decision was made. He was taking Basadict and they would leave soon.

A light rain began to sprinkle the clearing.

Three days had passed since they left the camp. They were good days. Days that weren't filled with a sense of urgency to get somewhere or do something. They were heading to the coast but not in a hurry to get there. It was as if a cloud had been lifted from Tedashuit when he and Basadict walked out of the camp. He had left all the concerns of the camp behind and was determined to enjoy the trip and the company of his young charge. He was the closest thing to a son he would ever have.

Last night it rained all night, soaking them to the skin. Wet weather was common this time of the year; it rained every few days. Basadict sat on a fallen tree trunk by the fire, drying his clothes. His spirits had not been dampened in the least and he was just as excited as when they left. Looking up at the sky, Tedashuit could see it was clearing. Off in the distance the clouds were thinning and small patches of blue were visible. It was showing promise of a good day. They were near the coast so today they would be leaving the river, traveling through the woods to a cove where he knew a Buggishaman had settled. It was about a half day's walk from here.

He vigorously rubbed the stump at the end of his arm. It was the damp weather; it always gave him trouble. He knew the annoyingly persistent ache would be with him most of the day. Bad enough he had lost the hand but now he had to put up with this nagging pain every time it rained. Another reason to hate the Buggishaman.

Basadict pulled a long stick away from the fire and grabbed his shirt that was dangling from the end of it. "Dry enough," he announced. "Smells of wood smoke, but dry."

"Well, then I guess we should get going. The day will be half gone by the time we get there," declared Tedashuit as he tied the string around his bed mat and slung it over his shoulder.

Basadict pulled the shirt over his head, stomped out the fire, and followed Tedashuit into the woods.

The sun was high overhead in a rare cloudless sky when they reached the edge of the woods on the other side. From where he stood, Basadict looked out over a section of land that had been cleared by the Buggishaman. Small mounds of dirt ran the length of the field with space enough to walk between them.

"That's where the potatoes will grow," explained Tedashuit, pointing to the rows of dirt.

In the middle of the field sat a wooden cart with a single wheel at the front. A shovel was propped up in the cart on a wooden bucket that had fallen on its side. The ground followed a gentle slope down toward a small cabin near the shoreline. A narrow path wove around weather-aged boulders, leading to a wharf that projected out into the quiet water of the sheltered cove.

"I don't see a boat at the wharf," said Tedashuit softly. "That means the Buggishaman is not around. It should be safe to go down there."

"Where is the shed?"

"It's behind the cabin. You can't see it from here."

"Is he the only one that lives here?"

"I've only seen one of them when I've been here before."

"Is this where you got the prong?"

"Yes."

"There's smoke coming from the house."

"Yes there is, but he probably just left the fire in so he wouldn't have to start it when he gets back. He's most likely not gone too far. Maybe we will sit and wait here for a while to make sure no one is at the house."

"How long before the potatoes come through the ground?" asked Basadict as he pointed at the mounds of dirt.

"A few weeks."

"We should come back and get some then."

"We will," replied Tedashuit. "Nice of the Buggishaman to grow them for us," he grinned.

"I wonder where Aaduth and Jaywritt are?" said Basadict as he gazed out over the water beyond the cabin. "I wonder if Aaduth killed a monau yet? Wouldn't it be something if we ran into them here at the coast?"

"That would be something," replied Tedashuit, warily. They had been away too long, he doubted that they would ever see them again.

Basadict looked around restlessly. "I don't think there is anyone here," he said.

"I think you 're right," said Tedashuit, pushing to his feet with a soft groan. He stood there a moment, rubbing his back. Seemed like there were more aches these days, he thought. I guess that's a part of getting older.

"Let's make our way down there," he said. "Now remember what I told you. If you see the Buggishaman, run into the woods. You don't stop for anything, no matter what happens."

"I will," nodded Basadict.

"We 'll go as far as that wood-pile first," said Tedashuit, pointing at the firewood stack at the edge of the open ground. The long sticks of wood were stacked on end with their tips leaning against each other, forming a shape much like that of a mamateek.

"Why is it stacked that way?"

"Not sure. I think that's how they dry their wood to make it burn easier. They cut it into smaller pieces later."

"Looks like it could fall over any minute. All it needs is a good strong wind."

"That's a lot stronger than you think. You'll see when you get a closer look. Let's go."

They crouched down as they ran across the open field until they reached the tall stack of wood. Tedashuit peered around the logs. From here he could see the shed on the other side of the cabin. There was a small window in the end of the cabin facing them, just big enough for someone the size of Basadict to fit through. He watched the window for a few minutes but could see no movement inside.

The rickety shed door stood open, its rusted hinges squeaking as the swirling wind pushed it back and forth. The only other sound was the shrieking of a pair of seagulls arguing over some floating debris out in the cove.

Tedashuit decided they were alone.

They had to cross more open ground to reach the shed. They would be exposed with no protection. If they were caught out here in the open, they would be in trouble. That worried him a little, not so much for him but for the boy.

He turned back and smiled at Basadict, "Ready?"

Basadict nodded eagerly, a little too eagerly thought Tedashuit. He has no idea how dangerous these Buggishaman can be.

Tedashuit walked around the woodpile and started toward the shed with Basadict following close behind. He kept an eye on the cabin as they crossed the rocky ground, ready to run at any sign of movement.

They reached the open door without incident and Tedashuit began to relax a little. The little shed had no window so the only light was provided by the open door; but in the bright midday sunlight it was easy to see all the way to the back wall.

Tedashuit stepped inside, closely followed by Basadict. Basadict looked around him in wonder at all the treasure. At the back, several nets and coils of fishing line were stacked on the floor. Against the wall stood a number of rusty garden tools. Two boat paddles leaned against a dirty white sail that was wrapped around a long post. A shelf ran the length of one side with an assortment of bottles and cans filled with nails and bolts and other things he didn't recognize. Along the other side he spotted the source of the strong briny smell that had hit him when he first stepped inside. A long narrow bin that stood as high as his waist was pushed back against the wall with the cover tied open. Inside he could see rows of stacked salt fish. An open barrel, half filled with salt, stood next to it.

Basadict reached in, pulled a fish from the bin, and touched his tongue against it. The briny taste filled his mouth and he looked at Tedashuit excitedly.

"Good?" smiled Tedashuit.

Basadict nodded with a grin and slipped the fish into his pouch.

Tedashuit turned back to the side wall and picked up a can of long nails from the shelf. He was about to dump them into his pouch when a shadow filled the door. He turned and found himself facing the long barrel of a gun. A tall, bearded Buggishaman was peering back at him through the sight of his shotgun.

Basadict had his back to the door and was about to slip a second dried fish into his pouch when he noticed Tedashuit staring over his shoulder with a startled look on his face. Slowly, he turned and saw a large Buggishaman filling the doorway. The fish slipped from his hand and he backed against the wall beside Tedashuit.

The Buggishaman was angrily shouting something at them but Basadict had no idea what it was. He shrunk back, trembling in fear, unable to take his eyes off the barrel of the gun. He felt the rough boards pressing into his back. They were cornered and the Buggishaman blocked their only way out. He was going to kill them. Basadict was aware of the tear that had escaped and was slowly trickling down over his cheek. He was too scared to brush it away.

Tedashuit stepped in front of him, momentarily blocking his view of the Buggishaman. He whispered from the corner of his mouth, "Remember what I told you boy. Run."

Basadict looked at him. There was nowhere to run. The door was blocked by the angry Buggishaman. There was no possible way he could get past him, and he had a gun.

Tedashuit turned and looked into his eyes, nodded, and then without warning, he took a step forward, grabbed the barrel of the gun, and pulled. The explosion filled the small enclosure, blasting Basadict's ears and throwing him against the sail. He instinctively clamped a hand on each side of his head to try and stop the ringing as he slid to the floor. Looking around the room in confusion, he found Tedashuit laying on the rough wooden planks between him and the Buggishaman. Dark red blood sprayed from the gaping hole in his chest, soaking the leg of Basadict's trousers. He released his hands from his ears and rubbed them along his sides. His right hand landed on something wet. He lifted it up in front of his face and looked at it curiously. It was covered in blood, his blood. He must have been hit by the gunshot as well. He pushed up from the floor, leaving a red handprint behind. Leaning against the wall, he shook his head to try and clear his vision. He stumbled toward the light coming through the doorway and brushed past the Buggishaman who had let his gun drop to the floor.

Bursting into the bright sunlight, he squinted his burning eyes and turned toward the beach. It was closer than the woods and he would be able to get to the trees farther down the shoreline, he reasoned.

Basadict didn't look behind him. He just stumbled along with his hand pressed tightly against his bleeding side, expecting to hear another gun blast at any minute. His breath was coming in sharp gasps and his ears were still ringing. With every step, pain shot through his body. It was hard to think.

When he reached the end of the clearing, he turned and scrambled up the bank to the trees. At the treeline he stopped and looked back. The Buggishaman was standing by the door of the shed watching him. There was no gun in his hand. Basadict pushed his way through the low bushes and scrambled into the woods. He would find somewhere to hide for the night and try and find the river tomorrow. If he could find the river, he *might* find his way back home. He wished he had never come to the coast. He could have been safe at home, far away from the Buggishaman.

The searing pain in his side was forcing the tears from his eyes. At times it was hard to breathe, but he knew he needed to get deeper into the woods in case the Buggishaman tried to follow him. He noticed he left blood on the trees when he gripped them for support, but he couldn't help that. He just had to keep going, and he needed the trees to keep from falling.

As he continued to trudge through the woods, his thoughts turned to his friend Aaduth. He wondered if he ever caught that monau he had bragged about. That would have been something to see. He wondered if his friend was alright. He had been gone an awful long time. He wished Aaduth were here. He would know how to get out of this.

He knew Tedashuit had been killed. No one could have survived that blast. He had seen the terrible hole the gun had made. He wondered why the Buggishaman hadn't followed him. All the stories he had heard told of how the Buggishaman killed every Beothuk he saw. Maybe he saw I was shot and figured I would die anyway, he thought.

He wished his mother was here to help him. She would know what to do to stop the bleeding from his side.

He thought of his little sister Ebanthou. It would be nice to get a hug from her right now. It was getting harder to see through the tears.

Basadict wandered around for a while until the agonizing pain in his side finally forced him to stop. He slumped to the ground, leaned his back against the trunk of a spruce tree, and closed his eyes. His side felt like it was on fire and his stomach was roaring with a dull, angry hunger. He lifted his hand from his side and wiped it in the moss. Then he reached into his pouch, hauled out the dried fish, and began to eat. The more he ate, the thirstier he became. He wished he knew where the river was. He was so sleepy and couldn't force himself to get up. I will drink tomorrow, he thought as he fell over onto his side.

The throbbing inside his head was unbearable and he cried out in pain as he moved to look up to see where he was. A wave of nausea washed over him and he pressed his eyes tight against the sunlight that threatened sear away his eyesight. Lying there, waiting for the swirling pain and nausea to pass, he wondered what was happening to him. He had no idea where he was nor how he had gotten there. Try as he may, he just couldn't remember.

He had a terrible pain in his side and he felt too weak to move.

Squinting his eyes against the sun, he scanned the ground around him. Nothing was familiar. All was quiet. Where was everyone? Suddenly, he spied a shadow moving through the woods toward him. The closer it came, the surer he was that it was Aaduth.

"Aaduth, where have you been? You were gone so long, I thought I would never see you again," he said with relief.

At last help had arrived. Basadict reached out his hand toward his friend, but to his surprise, Aaduth began to disappear, dissipating into the air. Tears filled his eyes and he slumped over on the ground again. He realized it wasn't Aaduth. It was just a memory.

Another wave of nausea washed over him and he felt himself slipping away again.

Some time later he opened his eyes. His face was pressed into the moss and his nostrils were filled with the pleasant woodsy smell. He moved and the pain came roaring back. He tried again, taking care not to move too fast this time. He gradually pushed himself up until he was sitting with his back against the tree again. He felt a slicing pain in his side and looked down to see his shirt covered in blood. He carefully pulled the ragged cloth away from his skin where it had stuck to the open wound in his side. It made him grind his teeth and moan with pain as the torn cloth pulled free and dark blood oozed from the long cut. Lifting the shirt, he studied the wound. Blood had dried all around the deep gash, but touching the surrounding skin sent shooting pain up his side into his head. An angry red mark had spread from the cut halfway up his chest. It was tender to the touch.

Leaning his head back against the trunk of the tree, he shut his eyes tightly and tried to push through the staggering pain, struggling to recall what had happened. He thought about Tedashuit, but why? What did it have to do with him? Where was Mother? Why wasn't she here to help him? He tried to call to her, but all he could manage was a croaking whisper through his parched throat. Water…I need water, he thought. The river. I have to get to the river.

Despite the warm sunlight on his face, he felt chilled and he shivered uncontrollably. The shivering made the pain worse. It needed to stop.

Gritting his teeth, he pulled himself up the tree trunk until he was standing. The ground was spinning under his feet and he closed his eyes tight until the feeling eased again.

Pushing off, he turned and began to shuffle forward, toward the river. Somehow he kept going, holding to the trees as he walked, driven by his burning thirst. The river was somewhere just ahead. He would be there soon. He could imagine the cool refreshing water trickling down his throat, putting out the fire that blazed there. It would be so good.

A few minutes later he stopped and stared in bewilderment. There, just a few steps away, was his pouch propped against a birch tree. In frustration, he realized he had only managed to walk in a circle. Sobbing uncontrollably, he dropped to his knees on the hard forest floor, jarring the womb. He gasped as the pain exploded in his head and he tumbled into darkness again.

He opened his eyes. Suddenly he remembered Tedashuit and the shed. It all came flooding back; the Buggishaman, the deafening blast of the gun, Tedashuit collapsing on the floor, and the bullet tearing through his flesh. He had been shot. That's what had happened to his side.

He had heard the stories around the campfire how Shanadee had walked home through the bitterly cold winter night after being shot. She had been the same age as he was now. So why couldn't he do it? Why couldn't he figure out which direction to go in?

He wished his mother or Aaduth were here. Someone. He didn't want to be all alone; not now.

Staring at the moss that blanketed the ground between his hands, he thought it would be nice to just go to sleep here. Perhaps if he rested for a while, he thought; and then with no warning a new wave of blinding pain washed over him. He screamed in agony and he felt himself sliding into a deep blackness, from which he was sure he would never escape.

Chapter 8
1823

It had been a long day, a strange day. There had been more twists and turns in this day than any other since Andrew had landed on this island. Things had happened that he never dreamed he would see. One thing he knew with a certainty, this day's events would change his and Sarah's future, and for the better he expected.

After unloading everything from the boat, he and the boy had dug a shallow grave in the half frozen ground behind the potato garden. There, they had buried the boy's father. Before covering the broken body with earth, the boy had carefully placed his father's weapons in the grave with him. Together they had covered the grave with stones and then Andrew hammered a wooden cross into the ground to mark the site. Sarah had stayed in the house while all this was happening. Andrew wasn't sure if it was out of respect for the boy or just that she wouldn't have been able to get through it. He was glad she stayed away. It was a scene he wouldn't soon forget.

When they finished, the boy sat on the ground next to the fresh grave and wept. Andrew had moved away and tried to busy himself with other things to give the boy some space, but he found himself glancing periodically over his shoulder to observe the boy's grief. Each time he turned to watch the boy, he felt a stirring of emotions deep in his own soul. He couldn't imagine what he was going through and how utterly alone he must be feeling. He hoped, in time, he and Sarah would be able to fill some of that emptiness.

After some time had passed, he returned to the gravesite and stood quietly behind him.

"It's time to go," he finally said, placing his hand on the boy's shoulder. He felt the small shoulder stiffen beneath his hand and gave it a reassuring squeeze. The boy stood and began walking toward the woods.

"No, no," exclaimed Andrew. "It's time to eat," he said while making the motion of placing food in his mouth. He pointed toward the house and waved for the boy to follow him.

Aaduth stood there watching the Buggishaman. He wasn't afraid of him. If he had wanted to kill him he would have done it by now, and he certainly wouldn't have taken the time to bury his father. He seemed to be a kind man. He had never been told there were Buggishaman like this. He had always been taught to run away from them.

He hadn't eaten all day and he was getting hungry. The Buggishaman seemed to be inviting him back to the house to eat. It would be dark soon and he had no idea how to get back to camp. He hadn't paid much attention to the trail coming down to the coast. He had simply followed his father, relying on him to get them home. Now he wished he had been more observant.

What choice did he have? They seemed to want to feed him, not hurt him. Anyway, it would be a lot easier to travel tomorrow with a full stomach. He wondered what kind of food they ate beside monau.

He began to follow the Buggishaman toward the house.

Sarah watched through the small window at the back of the house as they approached. She clutched her worn, leather-bound Bible to her pounding chest, smiling from cheek to cheek with anticipation. She had prayed for a child for so long. Could this be the answer? she wondered. Maybe God had heard her; just like the Bible story of Abraham and Sarah she so often turned to, maybe God was answering her prayers too. She hoped so. Maybe she wouldn't have to wait till she was a hundred years old like them; she laughed aloud at the thought. If this was her answer, she was certainly going to make the most of it.

Since she had left the boat down at the beach, she had made herself busy cooking seal with carrots and potatoes from last year's harvest. The vegetable supply was getting low but they were close to planting season and soon would be able to fill the cellar again. Might need more this year, she thought; might have another mouth to feed. Wouldn't that be something.

She dropped the Bible on the bed and returned to the stove. The stovetop was crowded with the cook-pot, the bread, and an apple pie she had prepared since returning from the beach. I need a bigger stove, she thought.

She sniffed approvingly. Nothing smelled like it was burning. She was never happier than when she was surrounded by the smell of dinner cooking on the stove. It was what made the place a home. Now she might be blessed enough to share her cooking with someone other than Andrew. She heard their footsteps on the deck outside and turned toward the door in excited anticipation.

Aaduth stepped onto the deck behind the Buggishaman and came to a standstill as he sniffed the mouth-watering scents that spilled out through the partly open door. He had never smelled an apple pie before, but whatever that smell was, he knew he was going to enjoy it. After such a hard day, he was surprised to find a smile had crept across his face.

He followed the Buggishaman through the door.

He had never been inside a Buggishaman's house before. It was nothing like a mamateek. He stood there looking around him in wonder. The floor, the walls, and the ceiling were all made from wood. There was a bed raised from the floor, a table with chairs to sit on, and a metal stove in the centre of the room. There wasn't a hole in the roof for the smoke to escape. He wondered where it went. He turned and saw the cove through the large window. Reaching out his hand, he tentatively touched the glass.

Sarah stood near the stove with her hands wrapped in the flour dusted apron and watched him as he stepped into their home. She wanted to reach out and hug him but was cautioned by Andrew, who quietly and discreetly said, "Don't rush it Sarah. You don't want to scare him off. He's had a really tough day."

She knew Andrew was right but it was hard for her to restrain herself. After all, this was not just coincidence, this was her answered prayer. God had always planned this for her.

She watched him standing there staring around their home. She realized all this was new to him and she didn't want to break the spell. He's such a good looking boy, she thought. Her heart was racing inside her chest with excitement.

The small table was set for three. It was so full there was hardly room for their elbows. He won't go hungry tonight, Sarah thought.

"Get another chair from the deck," she instructed Andrew.

"I guess I'll have to get to work on a third kitchen chair," he announced as he returned with one of the outside chairs. "Going to be a lot of changes around here."

Sarah held one of the chairs out from the table and motioned to the boy to sit.

Aaduth watched them warily. He was still a little nervous. All this was so new to him. It was happening so fast. A part of him still wanted to turn and run from this place. These two were not bad people, he was sure of it, but he should be careful anyway. Of course, there was no reason he couldn't sit down and enjoy the meal; the food smelled so good. He was afraid his stomach might be leading him into a trap.

He looked at the Emamoose as she offered him the chair. He had never seen anyone smile so much. She kept wiping her hands in the apron. She looked as nervous as he felt. What did she have to be nervous about? he wondered. He decided to go for it and sat in the chair. As he took his place, she carefully pushed the seat into the table.

Now closer to the plate of food, his nose was filled with the delicious smell of the cooked meat. He couldn't wait any longer. He grabbed the slab of steaming meat in his hands, bit off a sizable chunk, and began to chew noisily.

The Buggishaman and Emamoose were sitting down now too, but they hadn't touched their food yet. He watched them curiously. They had their heads bowed and the Buggishaman began talking in their strange language.

When the Buggishaman finished they both opened their eyes and smiled at Aaduth. Then they picked up their knives and the other shiny tool laying next to the plate and began cutting the meat into small pieces before they began to eat.

Why are they doing that? wondered Aaduth. Using your hands is much faster.

He looked down at his plate and didn't look up again until everything was gone. This is the best meal I have ever had, he thought.

The smiling Emamoose pushed her chair back from the table and brought the pie over from the stove. She cut a large piece and dropped it on a second, smaller plate which she pushed in front of Aaduth.

Clearly this was the source of the strong smell that had hit him when he had stepped onto the deck. He was full already but the smell was overpowering and he had to have it.

The first bite filled him with delight. It was so satisfying he wasn't even aware of the juice that had dribbled down his chin and the chunks of apple that fell to the table as they squeezed out from between the crust he was holding.

Sarah laughed softly and handed the boy a spoon, showing him how to scoop up the loose pieces. Andrew looked on with amusement.

"You got your work cut out there," he smiled at Sarah.

Her quiet smile said it all.

Looking into her glistening eyes, he knew he had never seen her so happy.

He stood up from the table, went to the stove, and threw some wood onto the fire. It was getting dark outside so he lit the three large candles that were spread around the house and pulled a caribou skin down from the overhead rafters. He spread the skin on the floor near the stove. "You sleep here," he said slowly, motioning to the Beothuk boy. The boy left the table and went and sat on the skin. Just as Andrew expected, he had eaten so much that he was sleepy, and before long he had fallen asleep where he sat.

Sarah busied herself cleaning up the dishes while keeping an eye on the sleeping boy. Her mind was racing with all the plans she had for him, so much so that when she reached out for another dish she found nothing, having completed her daily chore in a complete daze.

She blew out the three candles and, using the faint moonlight coming through the large window, she went and lay down on the bed with Andrew.

She listened to her husband's soft breathing.

"Are you asleep, Andrew?" she whispered.

"Uh-uh," he mumbled sleepily.

"We have our boy," she whispered into his ear excitedly.

"Now Sarah," he whispered back in the dark, "don't get your hopes up yet. You have no idea if he will stay with us. You know he will most likely want to get back to his people."

"Everyone says there aren't many of them left, Andrew. He probably has no idea how to find them, if there are any to find. Besides, he is much better here with us."

"You don't know that."

"Don't I now?"

"How do you plan to keep him here? We can't just tie him up."

"I'll make it so good for him here he won't want to leave."

"That might work," Andrew conceded sleepily.

"How old do you think he is Andrew?"

"I don't know. Nine or ten, I s'pose," he murmured.

"He's tall isn't he."

Sarah was quiet for a while and then said, "I think I love him, Andrew."

"You don't even know him, Sarah."

"I know how I feel."

"Andrew."

"Andrew?" Sarah realized she had lost him to sleep.

Sarah lay there staring at the dark ceiling, listening to the sounds of the two of them sleeping. She could just hear his light breathing over Andrew's intermittent snoring. Her mind was racing with all the things she needed to do. So many things would be changing around here. She couldn't wait to get started. This was going to turn out to be the best thing that could have ever happened to them.

I'll call him John, she thought. John Foss. That's a good strong name. Andrew will like that. It was his father's name back in the old country.

I wonder what his Beothuk name is? Probably something I can't pronounce anyway. Guess I'll find out eventually.

I've got to start teaching him English right away.

I wonder if he would be in any danger from the other settlers if they find out he is here? I think I'll tell Andrew not to talk to anyone about him. It's better not to take the chance and put him in any danger. His skin is a little darker than ours, but not enough to notice. Once his English gets better we can pass him off as our son.

He's such a good looking boy. We'll have to get that red paint off him though. He'll have a good future with me and Andrew.

"Thank you God for answering my prayer," she whispered. "Thank you."

She knew she wasn't going to get much sleep tonight. But that's alright, I'll just listen to him sleep, she thought.

Outside, the night wind began to rattle some of the loose boards on the shed, trying to get its fingers underneath the seams and tear them free. Farther down on the beach, the waves were being pushed against the shoreline in a familiar rhythmic motion. The sound soon lulled her to sleep.

Chapter 9
1823

On the morning of the fourth day Sarah awoke to find him gone. At first she thought he was down at the wharf with Andrew, but when she looked through the big window she could see Andrew was alone. The caribou skin that John slept on was rolled up and all his things were gone. That was unusual. With growing apprehension that was leaving a horrible sinking feeling in her stomach, she stepped out on the deck and shouted to Andrew.

"Where's John?"

Andrew looked up. "He's gone," he shouted back. He climbed up onto the wharf from the boat where he was working and quickly walked back up to the house. He knew Sarah was about to be upset and he needed to be there.

When he reached the deck he saw the tears in her eyes just as he knew there would be. He had been expecting this all morning since he had watched John disappear around the point. He had been dreading this moment but he had known it was coming.

"Where do you think he's gone?" she asked with a tremble in her voice.

"I expect he's gone to try and find his people, Sarah. I told you this might happen."

Sarah stood there staring out over the water, wringing her hands.

"But why, Andrew? I did everything I could to make him feel at home. You know that," she sobbed.

"I know you did," he said, "but don't you think he would want to find his own people. His mother may still be back there somewhere. Perhaps he's got brothers or sisters."

Andrew watched another tear find its way down her cheek onto her lip. He wrapped his arm around her shoulder and held her tight.

"It'll be alright, love," he said gently. "He'll probably come back when he gets hungry. Where is he going to find food like yours?"

"Do you think he might, Andrew?" She looked at him hopefully through tear filled eyes.

"I do," said Andrew with confidence he didn't feel. He knew Sarah needed something to hold on to, and he supposed anything was possible. He didn't think there was any chance the boy would ever find his way back to his camp, but he must know the woods and maybe he could survive out there. He wasn't sure how this would end. "We have to give him his space and hope for the best," he said. "He'll be back when he figures out he's alone. Besides, I doubt if he can find his way back to their camp anyway."

"I hope so Andrew, I sure do hope so. I need that boy around here."

Aaduth had spent four days with the Buggishaman and Emamoose. They were good days with more than enough to eat and an abundance of kindness, especially from the one called Sarah. He was never cold and he was never hungry. She went out of her way to make sure of that.

Sarah was intent on teaching him words from the Buggishaman's language. The first words she taught him were their names, including the one she had chosen for him. She seemed to get so much pleasure when he mastered them. It made him smile how she laughed aloud at his success.

It was a good place, and it helped ease the loss of his father, but it was time he returned to his own people. His mother and sister would need him. He was all they had left. He needed to let them know what had happened to Father. Mother must be worried about them and wondering where they were. They had been gone a long time.

There were so few of the tribe left now. They needed all the help they could get just to gather enough food to survive. He must try and get back to the river camp. Mother and Linguitt were his responsibility now.

The sun had not yet turned the night to day, but lying there he could see the faint beginnings of sunlight through the front window. He had to leave before Andrew got up and that would be soon. He had taken some bread last night and stored it in his pouch. He knew Sarah wouldn't mind. In fact, he was certain that if she knew he was leaving, and she couldn't stop him, she would have laden him down with so much food he would not be able to carry it all.

This life these past four days was so different from the life he had known before. There was hardly anything to eat at the camp and he couldn't remember ever feeling full after finishing a meal before he came here. It hadn't been real cold in the mamateek, but it was always warm here in this wooden house; sometimes almost too warm to sleep.

Then there was the sickness. His father had talked about his mother and his sister on the trip down to the coast. He had heard the fear and frustration in his father's voice at not being able to do anything to help.

He wondered if they were still alright. Maybe it was already too late. Maybe the Buggishaman sickness had already taken them.

Thinking that he was all alone scared him and he tried to think of something else.

He wasn't sure how to get back to the camp other than find the Great River and follow it. He and his father had left the river before they reached the coast and travelled across country to reach the seashore, so he didn't even know what the place looked like where the river ended. It was a wide river near the camp so he figured it would still be big where it flowed into the sea. They had also travelled along the coast for a couple of days to get closer to the ice flow. He knew this was not going to be easy, so he'd better get started.

Quietly, he rolled up the caribou skin that Andrew had given him to sleep on and stored it against the wall. The soft noise of Sarah's sleep hadn't changed and Andrew's loud snores helped drown out any slight noise he might make. He picked up his pouch, slung it over his right shoulder, and silently crept across the floor, trying his best to avoid the floor boards that creaked the worst. He eased the door open just wide enough to slip through and gently closed it behind him. Outside he finally exhaled the breath he had been holding and it billowed around him in the chilly morning air.

Soft shafts of light from the distant horizon spoke of the approaching morning. Aaduth knew he had better get going or he would be caught leaving by Andrew.

He jumped from the deck and ran across to the shed. Inside he retrieved his hathemay, slipped it over his left shoulder with his pouch of arrows, and jogged up the rocky beach in the direction he and Andrew had come in the boat. He wanted to reach the point and get out of sight of the house before anyone saw him.

Just before turning around the point, he stopped and looked back at the house. He could just make out the figure standing on the deck in the early morning light. Thick smoke was pouring out of the stove pipe where Andrew had stoked the fire to warm up the house. He watched as Andrew held up his hand. He had hoped to avoid this. He felt guilty for leaving like this. They had been so good to him and he had just walked out. He knew Sarah would be upset and he wondered if he should go back. A jay shrieked in the trees near him, reminding him of the camp, and he turned and followed the rocky beach around the point, out of sight of the house.

Aaduth followed the coastline for three days. He saw no one. It was as if the place was completely uninhabited. He ate shellfish and the bread he had taken from the house. At night he made a bed at the treeline and slept under the stars. It was much colder than at Sarah and Andrew's place.

Most of the time he walked the beach, but at times he had to make his way through the woods to get from one cove to the next. Here the points separating the coves were defined by sheer rock faces thrusting up out of the sea, sometimes as high as two mamateeks, worn smooth and colored white by the waves that never stopped washing against them.

During the first day he crossed several coves that he thought might be the one where he encountered the washawet. He knew it had to be one of them because it hadn't taken them long to get to Andrew's place in the boat. The problem was nothing looked the same now that the ice and snow had gone, so he couldn't decide which cove was the right one. Anyway, he remembered he and his father had travelled along the coast for several days before reaching it so he was still a long way from the Great River.

On the second day he spotted a plump grouse wandering around the edge of the woods. He notched an arrow and followed it until he thought he had gotten close enough to take a shot. His first arrow stuck into the mossy ground next to the bird. Startled, it ran a short distance and fluttered into the lower branches of a bushy spruce tree. He walked closer to it this time and his second arrow knocked it from its perch. Using a long stick, he roasted it over an open fire that he managed to coax to life from the spark he had struck using the two stones he carried in his pouch. It tasted good, but inevitably reminded him of the food Sarah cooked and how much better hers' was. He wondered how she was doing and if she still smiled as much. He thought not.

During the third day he crossed several small streams that were emptying into the sea but nothing seemed to be big enough to be the end of the Great River. He hoped he was right to not follow them inland.

Early on the morning of the fourth day he saw smoke rising through the trees in the distance. His heart jumped for a moment. Could it be someone from his tribe? Had they come to the coast? It is more likely a Buggishaman this close to the sea, he reasoned. He quickened his step.

Staying in the cover of the trees, he followed the beach to the next point, whose rocky finger thrust far out into the water, marking the end of the cove. Instead of walking around the point, he decided to cross through the trees. At the other side he peered through the low brush at yet another small cove. This one was different. It had been claimed by a Buggishaman.

On the far side of the little inlet a wharf like Andrew's jutted out into the water with a boat tied to its end. A weather beaten shed that had once been painted red sat near the top of the winding path, leading from the wharf up the gradual incline to the house. Smoke rose lazily from the crooked, rusty stack sticking up through the grey papered roof. Behind the cabin Aaduth saw a Buggishaman working in the field. The land had been cleared down to the beach about halfway around the cove. There was no way to cross there without being seen.

Before leaving the last cove Aaduth had made up his mind that if he didn't find the river in the next cove he would stop this hike and return to Andrew and Sarah's cabin. There was no river here and his way was effectively blocked. It was time to go back. Perhaps he would return some other day and continue his search.

He was disappointed, but staying with Sarah and Andrew was not so bad. He figured Sarah would be happy to see him back. Andrew probably would be as well.

It had been a tough week, probably one of the longest Andrew had ever endured. The boy had been gone eight days now and Sarah had begun to give up hope, despite Andrew's reassurances. He had already accepted the fact that John wouldn't be returning. He just didn't know how he would ever get Sarah to the same point. She was sad and gloomy all the time. He had never seen her that way before, not even when they first landed on this island. She was strong. He had witnessed that many times over the past few years, but this thing was bringing her down. She didn't sing much these days. She spent her time reading the dog eared pages of her Bible and silently whispering her prayers. He had caught her staring at the *Births* page of the *Family Records* section the other day. He knew she had wanted to add John's name there but thought it was too early. He was at a loss as to what to say or do, so for the most part he stayed quiet.

Andrew tied up his boat to one of the corner posts at the head of the wharf. He finished tossing the last of the morning's catch up into the waiting bucket and then flipped the prong onto the dock. He washed down the inside of the boat with buckets of sea water, replaced the gang boards, and then climbed up the ladder. He thought he'd go up to the house and have a cup a tea before cleaning the fish. Sarah might need the company. He stood there a moment stretching his back to relieve some of the aches while gazing out over the water. The sun had been up a couple of hours and it looked like it was going to be a pretty good day. Other than a few wispy clouds on the horizon, the sky was clear, a pale shade of blue. Even though the air still had a little bite to it, there was a sense of spring. Soon the days would warm up and everything would begin to grow again.

Turning to leave and make his way up to the house, he caught a glimpse of movement out at the point. He put a hand up to shade his eyes from the sun and his face instantly broke into a smile. It was John.

"Sarah!" he yelled toward the house. "Sarah!"

The door crashed open and she rushed out onto the deck.

"What's the matter?"

Andrew simply pointed toward the approaching boy.

Sarah's hands flew up to cover her mouth. Andrew could hear her gasp all the way down at the wharf. She stumbled in her head long rush down the stairs, caught herself before she fell, and hurried down the path to the beach. They all met near the wharf.

Sarah had her arms outstretched and wrapped them around the boy, tears of joy flowing freely down her face.

Andrew stood and watched, grinning at John's obvious discomfort with Sarah's over-enthusiastic welcome.

When John was finally able to free himself they stood there in silence until Sarah grabbed his arm and pulled him toward the house.

"Let's get some food in you," she said. "You look like you are starved!"

"Good idea," said Andrew. "He probably hasn't had much since he left last week."

Andrew stood there at the end of the wharf watching the two of them as Sarah hurried John up the path to the house. He had listened to her quiet tears during the nights since the boy had left and it was clear to see how overjoyed she was to have him back. Things are going to be alright for her again, he thought with relief. It's good he decided to come back.

The two of them made quite a pair; him with his ochre-smeared tunic and Sarah with her long stained apron, which had come loose and was whipping around in the wind.

He smiled contentedly as he turned and walked back to the waiting fish. Forget about the tea, he thought. Let Sarah enjoy her time with him. I'd just be in the way.

Chapter 10
1823

Almost three weeks had passed since Aaduth had returned to Sarah and Andrew's place. Sometimes, when he let his guard down, he found he was starting to think of it as home. That always made him feel a little guilty. He still had family out there in the woods somewhere and he knew they did not have things as good as he did. Well, at least they have Tedashuit and Basadict to hunt for them, he thought.

It was late April and most of the chill had retreated from the air, now replaced by the damp fog that hung in thick curtains around the coastline. Most mornings he and Andrew took the boat out and hauled the fish nets. He couldn't understand how Andrew could always find his way home in the fog. He had no idea where they were once that thick haze had surrounded them and he always felt nervous until they returned to their wharf.

Even though Andrew talked all the time, they still had to use signs to fully understand each other. Sarah had been relentless in trying to teach him their language and he had picked up quite a lot of the Buggishaman words. He had even managed to teach Andrew a few of words from his native tongue when they were alone in the boat.

He was sitting on the end of the wharf with his legs dangling over the side watching the small fish swimming around the encrusted posts in the shallow water below. The mid-day sun had burned off most of the fog and the warmth of its rays on his back was making him sleepy. They had already cleaned this morning's catch and taken the fish up to the shed for salting. Andrew had gone up to the house while he had returned to the wharf.

In his mind, he was picturing the camp on the Great River. He wondered how they all were and if the disease had gotten his mother and sister. They had not been well when he and his father left camp and that was a month and a half ago. He turned and let his eyes wander past the house through the vegetable garden to the small pile of rock behind the little wooden cross that marked the spot where his father lay. With a heavy sigh, he turned back, looking down at his feet and the fish that swirled in the water below.

Father and he had been gone so long everyone at the camp would think something bad had happened to them and they would not be expecting them to come back; everyone except Basadict. Aaduth knew his friend would never give up hope. He was sure

Basadict would still be counting on getting the monau tooth. Out of habit, his fingers went to the tooth hanging on a string around his neck. Andrew had made the hole and threaded the string for him. He always kept it there as a constant reminder of his friend.

He wondered if he would ever see any of them again. He swiped his hand across his cheek to wipe away the single tear that had escaped and was trickling down his face.

He decided he had to make another trip to try again to get back there, but this time he would let Andrew and Sarah know what he was doing. Contrary to what he had always been taught, these two Buggishaman were good people and had shown him nothing but kindness since the first day he met them. If he couldn't find the camp this time, he could always come back and make this his home. He knew they would be happy about that, especially Sarah. It seemed she already considered him her son.

He heard Andrew's footsteps on the wharf behind him.

"Hey John, what are you doing there?" Andrew asked as he sat down next to him. Aaduth had already taught him his real name, but for Sarah's sake he continued calling him John.

"Me go," said Aaduth, pointing at his chest and then toward the point that marked the end of the cove.

Andrew looked at him thoughtfully and nodded, and then turned and stared at the blue line that marked the horizon far out in the distance. He had been expecting this. He knew the boy needed to find out what had happened to the rest of his family and the other members of the tribe. From his conversations with the boy, he had been able to figure out that there were thirteen of them left at the camp when John and his father began their journey to the coast.

He was terrified for Sarah that John wouldn't return if he reached the camp, but they had done all they could to make him feel a part of their family. The rest was up to John.

He had grown very fond of the boy and didn't like to think about not having him around, but he knew John would be restless until he found out about the others. He knew if he were in John's shoes he would want to do the same thing. Thing was, he and Sarah had never been so happy. Having a "son" had changed their lives so much.

"Yes," nodded Andrew reluctantly, "you go and find your people. But I hope you come back to us some day. You will always have a home here."

Aaduth smiled at Andrew. He liked this Buggishaman.

Andrew slipped his arm around John's shoulder and hugged him affectionately. "Now let's go up to the house and see what Sarah is baking. It smelled awful good when I was up there."

The next day, Aaduth left to try again. It was different this time. Now he was laden down with food and extra clothes. Sarah had piled so much together for him that he had to leave some of it behind. He could never have carried it all. If he had he would not have gotten past the first point. Of course maybe that was Sarah's plan.

It was almost midday and the morning fog had melted away. Light wispy clouds drifted lazily across the sky, occasionally blotting out the sun and casting long shadows that scuttled across the ground. It promised to be a good day to travel. He had decided to follow the path he had taken last time.

A few days ago Andrew took him in the boat and showed him the cove where the washawet killed his father. It was closer than he thought. At least he had something to go on now, although he still had no idea where he and his father had left the woods for the coast-line back then. He knew he still had to find the Great River if there was any chance of getting back to camp. That meant he had to find his way around the other Buggishaman's place.

Andrew and Sarah stood on the deck and watched him walk up the beach. Sarah occasionally wiped at her eyes with the corner of her berry-stained apron. Andrew stood close to her with his arm protectively around her shoulder. He found himself swallowing hard in an attempt to keep his eyes dry as well.

Just before John rounded the point, he turned and waved to them. Sarah waved back vehemently, now openly weeping. "Be careful and come back soon," she yelled, even though she knew he couldn't hear her at that distance.

"Do you think he 'll be alright?" she sobbed as she laid her head on Andrew's shoulder.

"He'll be alright," he replied as he tried to frame the picture of the boy in his mind.

Aaduth travelled faster this time. He was familiar with the path so he knew where he could take shortcuts without getting lost. Sarah had filled his shoulder bag with more food than he would need so he didn't have to take the time to find his own.

The only stop he made was on the first day in the cove where he had the encounter with the washawet. In his mind, he had already named it Washawet Cove. He took the time to build a small tower of rocks near the treeline to mark the spot and honor his father. He hoped he would be able to return here again someday, although he didn't know if that would happen if he did find the camp. But then he supposed he would make the trip to see Andrew and Sarah in the years to come.

He arrived at the other Buggishaman's place on the third day; a day earlier than last time. It was late evening and he decided to wait until the morning to make his way through the woods around the cleared land.

Taking care to stay out of sight, he sat on a large boulder behind some tall leafless birch trees and studied the Buggishaman's land on the other side of the cove.

It looked much the same as Andrew and Sarah's. The house was built a little way back from the beach, with a much used path winding down to a wooden wharf that extended out into the cove. A small boat like Andrew's bobbed in the evening swell at the end of the wharf. Behind the house the land was dug for a vegetable garden that ran up the gentle slope to the edge of the woods. At the side stood a stack of wood in the shape of a mamateek.

The land had been cleared of trees about halfway around the cove. He would have to leave the beach and make his way through the woods around the clearing to reach the next cove.

Although he had learned over the past month that Buggishaman could be kind and good, he suspected they were not all like Andrew and Sarah. Otherwise there wouldn't be so many stories of the bad things they did to his people. He decided he would stay out of sight of them like he had been taught. There was nothing to be gained by making contact with this Buggishaman. It would be best if the Buggishaman never knew he had been there.

On the other side of the cove smoke spiraled into the quiet evening air from the pipe jutting out of the roof of the house. It made him think of Andrew's place and a part of him wished he were back there in the warmth and out of the cold fog that was rolling toward him from the sea.

A lone blue jay flapped nosily overhead and found a perch in one of the birch trees near him. It sat there watching him for signs of food it might be able steal. Aaduth reached into his bag and pulled out a piece of Sarah's blueberry bread. Breaking off a small piece, he tossed it on the ground at the foot of the boulder. Without hesitation the jay swooped down, snatched the offering, and returned to its perch. Seconds later it began screeching at him for more. It reminded him of the day that his father had first talked to him about the trip to the coast; a jay had been squawking early that morning, causing Jeddilledt to yell back at it. That seemed so long ago now. Maybe he would get to see all of them again soon.

Out over the water the large, round, silver moon had cleared the horizon and was beginning its journey across the night sky. He tossed the bird one more morsel, returned the rest to the bag, and slid off the boulder. It was time to find a comfortable place to sleep for the night.

He awoke to yet another gray foggy morning. Even with the extra blanket wrapped around him, he was shivering. A gentle wind brought with it the salty scent of the low tide. He tore off a piece of Sarah's bread and coated it with a thick layer of blueberry preserve. Seemed like everything he did made him think of Andrew and Sarah. He sat there in the cold, munching on the bread and brooding.

He remembered how last night he had felt so full of hope of seeing the tribe again. But now the morning presented him with the cold harsh reality of the huge task he had set for himself. He had been worrying more and more lately that this trip was not something he could possibly ever finish. He hoped the Great River was in the next cove because he didn't know if he wanted to go much farther. He knew that he and his father had travelled cross country and then down the coast after leaving the Great River, but he had already passed the place where they had fought the washawet so it shouldn't be too much farther, he reasoned. He wished his friend Basadict were here with him. It would be a great adventure then, and not the insurmountable challenge it felt like now. Funny, he hadn't thought much about Basadict lately. Maybe he had it a little too good at Sarah and Andrew's.

Fact is, Basadict is one of the big reasons he was taking this trip in the first place, he reminded himself. He missed the good times they had back at the camp. All their excursions in the woods together and those lazy days they just sat by the river dreaming of what they would do when they grew up, he wanted that again. He remembered the stories they would repeat to each other about Shanadee, Nonosabasut, and the other great warriors they had never gotten to know. Basadict was more than just a friend, he was more like a brother. Perhaps he could bring him to meet Andrew and Sarah sometime. He would love for Basadict to meet them.

"Well, I'd better get a move on or the day will be half gone," he said aloud as he shook his head to bring his thoughts back to the present. He shoved everything back into the shoulder bag Andrew had given him and pushed himself to his feet.

He walked back to the boulder he had been sitting on yesterday, to check out the Buggishaman's land one more time before entering the cove. The first thing he noticed was the boat was gone from the wharf. He turned and scanned the sea but couldn't see anything through the fog that blanketed the coastline. He stood there in indecision, wondering if it was safe to just follow the beach or was there someone else in the house.

After a few minutes he decided to take the safe approach and make his way around the land through the woods. It would take longer but there was no point in risking unnecessary contact. Keeping as close to the treeline as he could, he walked along the rocky beach, picking his way through the driftwood left by the high tide while keeping a watchful eye on the water on his left for any sign of the Buggishaman. When he reached the place where the land was cleared he left the beach, pushed through the tangle of low brush, and entered the woods. The trees were only beginning to bud and hadn't received their cloak of summer leaves yet, making it possible to see for some distance. If it had not been that way, he probably would never have seen the bag. He spotted it out of the corner of his eye to his right and he turned off his path to check it out. As he got closer it suddenly clicked, he recognized that bag, and without a thought a single word escaped his lips. "Basadict!"

It was his. He would recognize it anywhere. The two familiar feathers he always dangled from the strap – one black and one blue – were unmistakable, and the way he had cut the fringe, the pattern of one small and two large. What was it doing out here?

It was sitting there propped against the base of a birch tree with a partially eaten dried fish next to it. When he picked it up, he felt dampness on his fingers as they touched the back. Turning it over he saw the partially dried blood and his heart skipped a beat. Where was Basadict? What had happened here? He must be hurt.

He spun around and peered through the trees but could see no sign of his friend anywhere.

"Basadict," he called. "Where are you?"

"Basadict!" a little more anxiously.

"Basadict!" a little louder.

He stood there clutching the bag in silence, listening, scanning the woods all around him. The only sound was the chirping of song birds he had frightened in the trees overhead. His heart was beating wildly as he imagined all sorts of terrible things that could have happened to his friend. He had to find him.

He reached up and hung the bag on a high branch and moved out, working his way through the woods in a circle, calling Basadict's name. At first he rushed, half ran, driven by his urgent need to find him. Then the realization that he might miss him pushed its way to the front of his mind and he slowed to a walk, carefully scanning the ground around him. Each circle he made around the tree was bigger, widening his search.

He had waded across the narrow brook for a third time and was nearing the end of this circle when his shout alarmed a group of crows who flapped nosily into the air, loudly screeching their annoyance as they flew. Aaduth whirled around in their direction and saw him, lying on his side, curled into a tight ball, facing away. Dodging around the bigger trees, he ran to his side and dropped to his knees on the moss-covered ground. Basadict's side was a mess of blood and torn flesh that he had tried to cover with his hand. Aaduth could see this was bad. He crawled around Basadict so he could see his face. Tentatively, Aaduth reached out and touched him; a low moan escaped Basadict's lips but his eyes remained firmly shut.

"Basadict," he said softly, "what happened to you?"

There was no response.

"Basadict," he leaned closer and tried again. "It's Aaduth. I'm here."

Nothing.

Aaduth bent over his friend and looked closer at the terrible wound in his side. Carefully, he lifted Basadict's blood-caked hand and gently raised the saturated, tattered tunic. Underneath, he saw the deep gouge of raw flesh that was still oozing dark watery blood. The smell of death made him gag. He gasped in dismay as he let the tunic slip from his fingers. He had no idea what to do. He was terrified and lost. This was not something that could be fixed.

Aaduth released Basadict's hand, sat back, and leaned his back against a tree. His stomach was rolling and his face felt flushed. He bent his head and closed his eyes, desperately fighting the nausea. Fear was rising in him in cresting swells and he looked around wildly for an escape. He needed to run away from this now.

Basadict moaned again. Little bubbles of red foam dribbled out the side of his mouth.

Aaduth shuddered, but it was enough to bring him back.

Water. He should get water for Basadict.

Jumping to his feet, he ran back to the stream to fill his water pouch.

He shuddered again as he waited for the pouch to fill. His hand was shaking uncontrollably. The enormity of all this was pressing down on him, threatening to suffocate him. He tried to concentrate on breathing slower and it seemed to help a little.

Water spilled from the pouch onto his leg as he ran back to Basadict. He realized he hadn't pushed the plug back in but he was close now and it really didn't matter.

Dropping to his knees, he dribbled the cool water on his friend's parched lips. Then he spilled some into the palm of his hand and washed it over Basadict's feverish forehead.

Basadict's eyes opened a little. "Water," he croaked through his dry throat, immediately followed by a scream of agony.

Tears filled Aaduth's eyes, blurring out the horrific scene before him. He wiped them away with his sleeve. He had to be strong for his friend. He had to be strong for both of them. It was all he had.

Basadict was still again. His ragged breathing was the only sign he was still alive.

Aaduth thought of Sarah. She would know what to do to help him. She was too far away and he could not leave Basadict. He had to do this alone. He was so afraid.

He lay down on the ground next to Basadict and placed his lips close to his ear.

"It's Aaduth, Basadict. I've come to help you. I have the monau tooth I promised you. It's here on my neck. Father and I had a great adventure. We were attacked by a great white washawet, one of those from the frozen land."

He paused, knowing that the next thing he would have to tell his friend was of the loss of his father. For a moment he considered skipping that part but then the vivid scene from that day filled his mind and he knew he had to share it. Swallowing heavily, he wiped a tear from his eye and continued.

"…it killed Father…" he said in a low voice, but soon his story picked up again. "You'd never believe what happened next. I was rescued by a Buggishaman. Imagine that Basadict, a Buggishaman. He even helped me bury Father. His name is Andrew and he has an Emamoose called Sarah. They are really good people. I live with them now. It's great, especially Sarah's food. I have some here in my bag. I am going to take you to see them when you are better. Can you hear me Basadict?"

"Aaduth? Is it you?" mumbled Basadict through dry chapped lips.

"Yes, yes, Basadict," answered Aaduth excitedly.

Basadict had gone quiet once more.

Aaduth held his breath, waiting for Basadict to speak. But he had slipped away again.

Aaduth waited, and continued to wait as the morning marched on.

From time to time he would wet Basadict's lips with the cool water. He pulled Sarah's blanket from his bag and spread it over his friend. The day was getting warmer but Basadict's whole body shook as if he were too cold.

Sometime later Basadict groaned and opened his eyes. He seemed to be staring not at Aaduth but past him. Curiously, Aaduth looked over his shoulder. There was nothing there but trees.

"It's me," he said.

Basadict nodded painfully. "How did you find me?" he whispered.

"I was heading back to the camp."

"I can hear you, but I can't see you," he said weakly.

"You're hurt. What happened to you?

"Where am I? Why is it so dark?

"We are in the woods at the coast. Do you remember what happened?"

"No," he gasped as another pain forced him to draw up his legs and he slipped away again.

Aaduth went back to the stream and refilled the water pouch. He returned and sat next to his friend. It seemed Basadict was gone longer this time but eventually he spoke again.

"No point going back to camp."

"Why?"

"Your mother, your sister, and Shanawdithit are gone."

"Gone where?"

"They had the Buggishaman's coughing disease so they left camp to try and save the rest of us. We never saw them again."

"Where did they go?"

"Don't know. Coast, I think. I need a drink," said Basadict painfully.

Aaduth slipped his hand under Basadict's head and gently lifted it while placing the pouch on his lips. Basadict drank too fast, choked, and spit most of it back up. It was mixed with blood. Aaduth felt Basadict's neck go limp and he was gone again. He lowered his head back to the ground.

Aaduth leaned back against a tree and cried out in anguish. Angrily, he pounded his right fist on the ground. It seemed that his friend had been here just a couple of days. If only he had come earlier, maybe he could have helped him.

Aaduth sat with his back to the tree and his arms across his drawn up knees. He rested his head on his arms and let the tears flow. He knew his friend was dying and he was helpless to do anything about it. His heart felt as if it was torn inside his chest. He moaned softly to ease the pain.

After a while, he raised his head and looked around. He wondered what had happened to Basadict. He must have been shot, probably by the Buggishaman whose land he was trying to get around. He would not have been here alone, but who was he with, and where were they? Maybe they were somewhere around here as well.

He decided he had better take a look around. Maybe the other person was hurt and needed help; but he wasn't sure he should leave Basadict alone. He should be there when Basadict opened his eyes again.

Aaduth leaned his head back against the tree trunk and closed his eyes. He needed to think. He swallowed hard against the fear that was crawling up inside his chest. He wanted to throw up. This was too much. What was he supposed to do?

His mind went back to the stories he had heard so often repeated at the campfires. His father always told him stories of his aunt Shanadee and how she had survived so many encounters with the Buggishaman. His father had always seemed to be so proud of her. He wondered what she would do right now.

The more he thought of the stories the calmer he felt. Maybe her spirit was here helping him. He remembered the stories of the moisamadrook and anxiously looked around him. Without their summer coat of leaves the trees did not provide much cover. He could see a long way through the surrounding woods. Nothing moved except the birds. It seemed he was alone.

Pushing to his feet, he stood with one hand on the trunk of the tree. He decided he would search the woods to see if he could find another member of the tribe that may have been with Basadict. He would try to stay close enough to hear Basadict if he spoke.

He was feeling better now. The jumbled thoughts were making more sense. He was breathing easier and he had a plan.

Basadict mumbled softly.

Aaduth had to lean his ear close to Basadict's mouth to hear what he was saying. Most of it didn't make sense and a lot of it wasn't clear. He did hear the names Tedashuit and Aaduth, or at least that is what it sounded like. It sounded as if Basadict was getting weaker.

Aaduth looked around helplessly. "Why?" he moaned aloud. This is not how he was supposed to be reunited with his friend.

He changed his mind. He was not going to leave his best friend, not when he needed him most. Even though he couldn't do anything to help him, he could at least be there for him. He knew he would want Basadict to do that for him. He carefully tucked Sarah's blanket around his friend's still body and waited.

The crows had returned and were roosting in the higher trees, watching with their beady black eyes. Aaduth eyed them angrily.

He considered shooting them from the trees. He knew they were here for his friend. That's what they always did. Filthy crows.

The sun had passed overhead and had started its journey down the other side when Aaduth opened his eyes. He looked around guiltily. The warm sun had lulled him to sleep. It seemed that Basadict had not moved. He hoped he hadn't said anything and no one was there to hear it. I would have heard him if he spoke, he reasoned.

He took a long drink of the lukewarm water in the pouch and made his way to the stream to refill it. He splashed the cool water over his head to wash away the lingering sleep and returned to Basadict's side.

Basadict was moaning softly again. Using his hand, Aaduth dribbled the cool water on Basadict's face. He stirred again and tried to move, but immediately stopped when the pain made him cry out.

"Aaduth. You're here!"

"Yes, Basadict, my friend, I'm here."

"But how, why? You were at the coast with Jaywritt."

"Yes, Basadict. I found you here. You are hurt."

"I was shot, Aaduth," he moaned as the pain wracked his body once again. He closed his eyes and waited for it to pass.

This time he didn't slip away.

"The Buggishaman shot me," he said weakly. "I need a drink."

Aaduth placed the pouch on his lips and let him sip only a little this time.

"He killed Tedashuit, Aaduth."

"Where?"

"Back there in the shed. I escaped or he would have killed me too."

The thought occurred to Aaduth that Basadict really hadn't escaped, but he pushed it out of his mind.

Basadict painfully lifted his hand and clutched on to Aaduth's as a new wave of agony crested over him. For a moment his fingers dug into the flesh of Aaduth's hand and then all his strength seemed to drain from him. His fingers released and his hand fell back down to the ground. He gave a tortured gasp as he struggled for breath and then fell silent.

Aaduth looked at him in fear, watching for movement. But for the red trickling down his chin, there was none. He had never seen anyone die like this. His father's death had been quick. He had not had to watch him suffer like this. He felt an ache, as if he knew the body before him was empty and his spirit was gone, but he had to know for sure. He placed his hand on Basadict's chest and felt no movement. Leaning close, he stared at his friend's face. Basadict was no longer breathing. Aaduth began to cry.

No longer afraid of hurting him, Aaduth pulled Basadict's head onto his lap and let his tears wash his friend's face. The dam burst and all the emotion he had been suppressing this long morning rushed out in a torrent of tears.

Time passed and the river ran out, he was just left with the dry sobs. He knew he had work to do to protect his friend and get him ready for the journey. Before lifting Basadict's head from his lap, he transferred the monau tooth from his own neck to his. Then he gently laid his friend's head on the ground and pushed himself to his feet.

Aaduth took a long drink from the pouch and then went and retrieved Basadict's bag from where he had hung it early this morning.

The ground was too hard to dig so he cleared away as much of the moss and undergrowth as he could next to Basadict. While he worked, he talked to his friend.

"I'm sorry I didn't get here a day earlier. Things might be different now if I had. I will never forget you Basadict and I will visit this place often. I wish you could have met Sarah and Andrew. They are good people. I will be returning there and will make a life with them. There is no point trying to get to the camp if my family is gone, especially now that you are gone as well. I will always miss you, my friend."

Once he had a big enough space cleared he dragged Basadict, as gently as he could, turned him on his side, and swivelled him to face the sunrise. He laid out the contents of the bag next to him and began to gather all the stones he could find.

He spent the rest of the day bringing rocks from the beach until he had him completely covered. Finally, he lay down next to the rock pile in exhaustion and slept.

Chapter 11
1823

Jeddilledt's body was wracked with another spasm of uncontrollable coughing. It seemed every muscle screamed in agony with each episode. A drum was pounding inside his head and his laboured breathing was raspy and dry. The salty taste of blood rarely left his mouth. He was so weak and tired from the unrelenting cough he barely had enough strength to sit up. Shivering, he tried to keep warm by huddling up in a dirty, tattered caribou skin blanket. His cramped, aching fingers held the blanket tight to his body as he fought off the waves of nausea that rolled in his empty stomach. He hadn't eaten anything for so long his body was as thin as the blanket he clutched so desperately. His body was as confused as he was. His growling stomach was begging him to eat something while the bitter taste in his mouth reminded him that if he ate it wasn't going to stay down.

What was the point anyway? He was the only one left and he knew it wouldn't be long before he would begin his journey to Gossett (land of the dead), just like everyone else in the tribe had. He looked around the mamateek at the still bodies that lay around him. The next spasm hit.

It had been three months now, or maybe it was four, that Jaywritt and Aaduth had left for the coast. He was no longer sure of the passage of time and he was easily confused by it, but he knew months had passed. They had never returned. He often wondered what had happened to them. It had to be something bad or they would have been back by now. They must have run afoul of the Buggishaman. Jaywritt would never abandon his tribe.

Jeddilledt remembered when Jaywritt was just a chubby little toddler following his sister Shanadee around camp. He had watched him grow into a strong young man; a young man who, after losing his sister and so many others of his family, had quietly assumed the leadership of the band. He had been the one who kept the little band together, but when he didn't return there was no one to take the role, at least no one had any desire to take it. They had sort of retreated into their individual mamateeks and just kept to the company of their own families.

Little did they know at the time that the Buggishaman's coughing disease had crept into the camp even before Jaywritt left for the coast, striking Jaywritt's daughter first. It hadn't been long after that the girl's mother began showing signs of the disease. He remembered that dark day when Shanawdithit had led her adopted mother and sister into the forest. They too had never returned. He suspected they had died out there in the woods somewhere. They wouldn't even get a proper burial. How would they make the journey to the land of their ancestors?

After the three women had left, those remaining in the camp had burned Jaywritt's mamateek. That had not stopped the disease, maybe slowed it down for a while but that was all.

It had been over a week since they had burned down the diseased mamateek and all had seemed well; then he and Laddiwett, his wife, started coughing. He remembered how he shrugged off Laddiwett's concerned look at the time. It hadn't seemed too serious at first, but after Basadict and Tedashuit left for the coast, it seemed to move a little faster through his mamateek and soon his daughter Middadewann began to show symptoms as well. Little Ebanthou was the only one in the family who didn't seem to be affected.

Everything seemed to happen faster after that.

Then just the other day Langnon had shouted across the clearing to tell him they were leaving as well. He was the only hunter the band had and Jeddilledt knew his going would leave them without any way to get fresh food; but he understood his son's reasoning. He was just trying to protect his young family from the cursed disease.

He remembered Laddiwett had harsh words for Langnon and what he was doing, but Jeddilledt knew if he were in his place he would do the same to protect his family. His wife was just scared.

It had not been a happy parting of ways. Laddiwett had refused to leave their mamateek to say goodbye. Langnon had left behind what little food he could spare and then walked out of the clearing with his son Jiggameel, his wife Godabonyee, and her sister Hanawadet. Jeddilledt had stood there with a blanket tightly wrapped around him and watched his future disappear into the forest. Tears had trickled down his weathered cheeks, following the meandering lines that life had carved in his face over the years.

Standing there in front of the door to his mamateek, he waved a last goodbye to them as they turned the corner in the trail that would take them downriver to the coast. He knew with a certainty this was the last time he would see his son. They had avoided direct contact once the disease had invaded Jeddilledt's mamateek but at least he saw his son in the clearing from time to time.

He remembered standing there staring after them until the chill of the early spring crept underneath his ragged blanket and drove him back inside. There was a time that it would not have bothered him at all but at that moment the cold seemed to be able to penetrate deep into his very bones.

Looking back, he knew it was the Buggishaman's coughing disease that had been eating away at his body.

Laddiwett had been the strong one. She had continued to prepare their food and care for him and their daughter as the disease progressed. He had spent his time gathering wood for the fire. He had known the day would come when he would be too weak to do it anymore.

When Middadewann could no longer muster the strength to care for little Ebanthou it was Laddiwett who stepped in. She fed her and mended her worn clothes. At night she would sing to her and tell her happy stories. She did her best to keep fear at bay despite knowing death had moved in and lurked in the shadowy places of the mamateek, waiting to claim the few who remained in their tribe.

The disease was strong and death does not like to lose. The sickness appeared to move faster in Laddiwett. One day he had seen her spitting blood into the fire and the next morning she didn't get up from where she slept. That must have been about three days ago, he thought.

He had managed to wrap her and move her to the back of the mamateek. He had planned to bury her outside but there was no one to help him and he found he wasn't strong enough to do it himself.

His daughter, Middadewann, lay on her blanket, unable to even look after herself, much less little Ebanthou. Yesterday

Middadewann's violent coughing fits ceased and she no longer moved.

He had managed to keep the fire going even though death hovered over him, constantly watching him, patiently waiting for him to get weaker. Death did not scare him; in fact, he would welcome it now if it wasn't for little Ebanthou. He gave her dried meat to chew on but he had no appetite himself. He would leave whatever food was left for her. It was no longer of any use to him.

Sometime the next day little Ebanthou must have wandered off and he couldn't muster the strength to look for her. He had managed to crawl to the door and peer out into the clearing. There was no sign of her and when he called her name there was no answer. She was only five. He knew she had no chance of survival but there was nothing he could do for her. He tried not to think of her wandering around out there in the cold, all alone and hungry, desperately needing her mother.

Memories, some clear and some jumbled, began to flood into Jeddilledt's mind. It was as if his life were being played out for him in his head. He had heard from others that this is what happened at the end. He was old now; older than any Beothuk usually lived. He had lived a long life. Why had that happened? he wondered. He had been there when most of the tragedies had hit the tribe. How had he escaped so long?

He remembered the night so long ago when Shanadee had stumbled back into camp after hiking through the freezing cold from the pond where her father had been shot. He had listened to her tale of the encounter with the Buggishaman and his gun. He remembered thinking at the time, it would be better for the Beothuk to avoid them altogether.

Later he accompanied Beeroute to help bring Shanadee's father, Nanolute, home. The wild winter storm that assailed them on their journey back to camp should have been sign enough that the spirits wanted them to avoid the Buggishaman. Instead, they took it to mean the spirits were angry with the Buggishaman and revenge was necessary. It turned out it wasn't the right decision.

He was there with Shanadee when she took her revenge on the Buggishaman called Tom Rowsell. In the ensuing retaliation for that act Jeddilledt had lost his first wife, leaving him alone with two young girls, Demasduit and Middadewann.

He huddled a little closer to the dying fire and weakly pushed a few of the remaining sticks into it. He was shivering uncontrollably. He thought he saw Jaywritt at the door but when he squinted his eyes the smoky figure he had smiled at drifted up and out the top of the mamateek.

His mind went back to their trip up the Great River into the interior. After the Buggishaman's fatal raid on their camp they had all decided it would be best to join the Beothuks who lived at the Great Lake. He could still see the horrible scene in his head when young Serondius went over the falls. Her mother's anguished screams sometimes came to him in the night. He remembered sitting on the river bank with his arms wrapped around his two young daughters after that. That had been a sad day; one of many.

Things had been a lot better once they arrived at the Great Lake. They were far from the coast and the threat of the Buggishaman. With the larger community, life had become normal again. He remembered being happy there. It was a safe place for his girls.

Jeddilledt glanced up from the fire. The wind was lightly brushing the leaves of a birch tree against the side of the mamateek. The sound, which would have at one time lulled him to sleep, was now more like a sigh of sadness, as if the world around him could feel the heaviness of his heart. He turned back to the fire.

Five years after arriving at the Great Lake he met and married Laddiwett. She was in the group Nonosabasut had brought in from the northern part of the island. She was a good woman, strong-willed, but a good fit for him. Life had gotten better for him after that. It had been easier with her there to help with the two girls.

One year after they married Laddiwett gave him his son, Langnon. They left the main camp then and moved to the far end of the lake. There had been sightings of the Buggishaman on the river closer to the Great Lake and Jeddilledt wanted to make sure his family was away from danger. He continued to believe avoiding contact was the best protection for them.

Because of that move he had avoided the meeting with Bukn and his Buggishaman soldiers. He only learned about it later when the fleeing group of Beothuk reached their camp and related the story of killing the two soldiers. Having somehow fallen into the storyteller role for the band, he had told the story so many times at the campfire that sometimes he forgot that he wasn't actually there.

It was darker outside now. He must have fallen asleep or maybe he had passed out. The fire was dying. He threw what remaining wood he had on the glowing embers and watched as the dry sticks ignited and tiny flames flickered to life. The silence was broken by the popping and crackling of the burning wood. His world had been reduced to the warm fire there in front of him, and the only movement was the dancing shadows on the walls of the mamateek that surrounded him. He wondered where Ebanthou was.

His mind drifted back to his children. His oldest girl, Demasduit, had married Nonosabasut, who had become chief of the Beothuk at the Great Lake. Nonosabasut had been good to Demasduit, but he had the ugliest face Jeddilledt had ever seen. The deep battle scar that cut through his lip and chin was not easy to look at, but Jeddilledt had discovered he was a gentle man underneath it.

Three years after Demasduit's wedding his son Langnon married Godabonyee and his grandson Jiggameel was born. Jiggameel was seven now and that's how he would remain in his memory. He hoped that their leaving the camp saved their lives, but he would never know.

He was alone with only his memories to keep him company. Somewhere close by the lonely howl of a moisamadrook pierced the silence. It reminded him of Shanadee. She had always said her father's spirit had come to her in a moisamadrook. He wondered if it was him howling into the night, or maybe it was Shanadee, or maybe it was just a moisamadrook.

He wasn't at the main camp when Shanawdithit had returned with the horrible details of Shanadee's murder but he knew the story well. He wondered how the Buggishaman could kill like that. It was as if they didn't think of the Beothuk as people. He wondered if they all felt that way.

The moisamadrook howled again. Jeddilledt shivered. Perhaps it was the sound of death coming. However, it was coming, he could feel its dark presence nearby. He looked at the still forms of his wife and daughter lying there in the deepening shadows. He wondered how long they had been there. Must be a while, he thought, because the mamateek was filled with the smell of death. Why couldn't he remember?

He thought again of his eldest, Demasduit. He hadn't been there when she was taken by the Buggishaman and her husband Nonosabasut and his brother Kirradittii were killed. At the time he was living farther up the Great Lake in a smaller camp with the rest of his family. They did move back to the larger camp shortly afterwards. That seemed so long ago now.

At least the Buggishaman Bukn had brought her back so they could give her a proper burial with her husband and their infant baby.

If all the Buggishaman were like Bukn we might have made it, he thought. He was a good man and tried to help them.

He lay back on the ground as close to the fire as he could get. He was chilled and too tired to cough anymore. He needed to start his journey. His ancestors were waiting for him. Staring up at the smoke slowly drifting out through the top of the mamateek, he thought he could see their faces in the swirling cloud.

Chapter 12
1823

"We can't stay here," she said angrily.

Langnon looked at his wife. He had expected this but he still wasn't ready for it. "Why can't we stay, Godabonyee?"

Glancing at her sister for support, she replied, "Look at them Langnon. You know they have the Buggishaman's coughing disease. If we stay it's only a matter of time before the rest of us get it. Have you looked at your father lately? There's nothing left but skin and bones. I don't think he's eaten in days."

"You and your sister and Jiggameel have not had any contact with them. We've been very careful about that."

"You've had contact!"

"They're my parents. I can't just abandon them. They're sick. The fact is I have not had much direct contact since we suspected the disease was in their mamateek. You know I have not been inside the mamateek."

"You have to make a choice, Langnon. You can leave and give Jiggameel a chance or stay here and die with your parents. I've made my choice."

"You know they won't make it if I'm not here to hunt food for them. There is no one else. You know that Godabonyee."

"Do you really think they will make it if you stay?"

"Probably not," he replied sadly.

Godabonyee crossed the dirt floor and put her arms around her husband. "I know this is hard, Langnon, but we have to try and save the rest of our family. This is no different than when your mother sent Shanawdithit, Doodlebewshet, and Linguitt away. That was to try and protect the rest of us."

Langnon looked down into her eyes. "I wish it weren't true, but I know you are right," he whispered.

She saw the tear floating on the rim of his lower eyelid and reached up and gently kissed his lips.

"We will stay a few more days. That'll give me time to hunt some fresh meat for them. Then we will leave and go to the coast," he decided and then pausing, he thought aloud, "What about Ebanthou?"

"What do you mean? You don't expect her mother will let her go with us do you?"

"Maybe, if she thought it would be for the best."

"She's been living in that mamateek, Langnon. She's probably got it too."

"I think we should offer."

Godabonyee took the two large grouse Langnon had been holding in his hand since he had entered the mamateek. She went to the other side of the fire and handed one to Hanawadet.

"We'll cook one for us and one for them," she announced.

Langnon sat by the fire, idly tossing more wood on it and watching the smoke as it slowly drifted up to the peak and out through the opening at the top of the mamateek. The disappearing smoke sort of reminded him of how fragile their position was. Just a few short weeks ago there were fifteen of them, now there were only eight, and he was about to take four and leave. He was deeply troubled by this. Why did he have to make this choice? It was not fair. He had to abandon some of his family to save the rest. How could this make sense?

He understood where his wife was coming from, but he wondered how much it was fueled by her dislike of her mother-in-law. He had always had to walk the fine line between his wife and his mother, and it hadn't been an easy journey. He hadn't been good at it; and more times than not, he was in trouble with one or the other. It was tough being a peacemaker between those two.

He became aware of Jiggameel watching him from across the room where the two women were preparing the birds he had just brought in. Lifting his hand, he beckoned for his son to come to him. A wide grin swept across the boy's face and he ran to his father's side and threw his arms around his neck almost knocking him over.

Langnon hugged his son affectionately. He wondered how much of the conversation Jiggameel had understood. Despite his inability to hear a sound since birth, he had adapted well and could understand much of what was being said by watching the lips of those speaking.

He knew the boy wouldn't be happy about moving. He was having enough trouble understanding why he couldn't visit his grandfather's mamateek anymore. He is only seven and he needs his grandparents around, thought Langnon.

Langnon thought of Jiggameel's early years. At first it had been difficult for the family to adjust to his hearing problem. It demanded so much extra time just to help him understand what was being said. He remembered the frustration of the constant repetition, but out of that came a deep connection with his only child. His hearing loss had somehow made him more special in Langnon's eyes and he knew there was nothing he wouldn't do to protect him.

As he rested his cheek on the top of the boy's head, he squeezed him a little tighter. He knew the future was very uncertain for him and life would not be easy. The important thing now was to get him far away from the disease that was killing his grandparents. The threat of being closer to the Buggishaman he could handle but there was no way to defend against the horrible coughing disease. To do this he would have to abandon his parents. He was torn with this decision. Godabonyee saw this clearer than he did. It wasn't that she had no feeling for Langnon's parents, well at least Jeddilledt, she just saw the protection of her family as the most important thing in her life.

Langnon had seen the disease at work in the tribe before and he knew the devastation it brought. He knew that in the end no one living in his father's mamateek would escape the disease. It was invisible and had a way of creeping from one person to the next. All those in close contact would be affected. Godabonyee was probably right, Ebanthou was living there with constant contact. He on the other hand had been careful to avoid it as soon as he knew.

If this were a wild animal like the moisamadrook he could fight it, but this threat he couldn't see. How was he supposed to fight this enemy?

They had lost the three women in Jaywritt's mamateek and now his father's mamateek was under siege. Langnon's mamateek was the only one left and he knew if they stayed they would not survive. He did not want anything to happen to his son, he thought, as he held him just a little tighter.

He felt the tear slide down his cheek and glanced across the mamateek. Godabonyee was watching him as she plucked the feathers from the grouse she was holding. It was as if she knew the struggle that was going on in his mind and she nodded and smiled reassuringly. She knew him well.

Tomorrow would be a hunting day and whatever food he found he would leave with his mother and father. He would also talk to his sister and offer to take Ebanthou. There was nothing he could do beyond that.

Tonight would be a sleepless night. He guessed there would be many more of those to come.

Chapter 13
1823

Shanawdithit reached into her shoulder bag and carefully pulled out the wrinkled and ragged birch rind. She gently unrolled it and looked at it again as she had so many times since they had left the camp. The charcoal line figures stared back at her, connecting her to those left behind. It reminded her of Jaywritt and Aaduth. She wondered what had happened to them.

They hadn't travelled far that first day and as the three of them sat in the makeshift shelter she had built they could see the telltale smoke rising above the trees in the distance. They knew it was their mamateek burning, closing the door on that part of their lives.

Shanawdithit had watched the smoke until it had all but disappeared. That black smoke was all that remained of her drawings that she had to leave behind. She remembered how her mother had proudly displayed them in their mamateek on a line strung across the ceiling. Her mother always made sure everyone who visited saw her daughter's drawings. She wished she could have taken them all but there was no room.

The three women huddled together and cried that night. The hopelessness of their situation was a burden that none of them could bear.

By the end of the second day the little food they had been able to bring with them was gone. Neither of them had the ability to hunt and it was too early in the year for berries. Snow still covered the ground in patches, making it feel as though, with each step, their feet were being sucked into the earth. The muddy paths made the going slow. It was impossible to walk without filling their moccasins with the muddy water. It was especially hard for Linguitt since she was too sick to walk on her own and had to lean on her mother's arm. The cold and wet only made it more miserable for her and she stumbled along in a trance. She cried most of the time now. They had to make frequent stops as she was often attacked by episodes of convulsive coughing. They were making slow and painful progress.

She knew Linguitt was very sick, and she felt sorry for her, but the constant whining was playing on her nerves. It never stopped. Their situation was bad enough without having to listen to that all day long.

Her eyes focused back on the birch rind in her hand. She looked at each figure in turn, picturing their face, remembering their voice. From her mamateek there was her adopted mother and sister, Doodlebewshet and Linguitt, who were sitting across the fire from her. Her Uncle Jaywritt had taken his son, Aaduth, and left for the coast a long time ago. Just the trace of a smile crossed her face as she remembered the stories she had been told of Jaywritt when he was a just a boy growing up under the watchful eye of her mother, Shanadee. He had idolized his big sister and wanted nothing more than to grow up to be just like her. He had been more of a father, than an uncle to her these past few years since her own father had been killed.

Old Jeddilledt and Laddiwett lived in the second mamateek with their daughter, Middadewann, and her two children, Basadict and Ebanthou. Laddiwett's brother, one-armed Tedashuit, also lived with them. Little Ebanthou was only five, the youngest in the camp. She reminded Shanawdithit of her sister, Mandolee. It was five years ago now since she lost them but the horrible scene was still burned in her memory. The brutal murder of her sister, her brother, and her mother, which she had witnessed, had left a dark empty place in her heart that had never been filled. There was little likelihood that it ever would.

The third mamateek was Langnon's. He shared it with his wife, Godabonyee, their seven-year-old son, Jiggameel, and Godabonyee's sister, Hanawadet. Jiggameel lived in a world without sound. Shanawdithit often wondered what that must be like, not to hear the chirping birds, the rattling of a brook, or even your own laugh. He had been deprived of so much yet he never appeared sad. Maybe some of it was the way Langnon doted on his son. There was nothing he wouldn't do for him.

She counted them off. Including her there were fifteen. Some of them were already gone and she feared more would be gone soon. She suspected that the Buggishaman's coughing disease had invaded Jeddilledt's mamateek as well. Middadewann had been showing signs the day they had left the camp.

"Will you put that away!"

She looked up at Doodlebewshet. In her watery eyes she saw only sadness. Linguitt lay next to her curled up in her tattered woollen blanket, stirring restlessly in her sleep. Just beyond her, drops of rain dripped from the tips of the drooping branches of the tall evergreen that they had huddled underneath for shelter.

"Why does this bother you Doodlebewshet?" she asked softly.

"Because they don't matter anymore," she replied angrily.

"They're our family, the only family we have."

"We will never see them again, besides they made us leave the camp. They sent us out here to die. What kind of family does that?"

"That's not their fault. You shouldn't blame them for that. It was the only way they could protect themselves from the disease."

"I do blame them. What are we supposed to do? You know we will die out here. We have no food and no one to help us."

"We will find something. We should reach the coast in a few days." In her mind she was remembering how she had heard Uncle Nonosabasut talk about the coming of this day; a day when there would be hardly any Beothuk left. He had been right and it hadn't taken as long to happen as he had expected.

She rolled the birch and slipped it back into her bag.

"This helps me remember them, Doodlebewshet. It's all we have left and I don't want to forget."

She added a little more water to the tin hanging over the fire, and then picked up a stick and stirred the tree bark. Other than some earthworms it was all they could find. It wouldn't help much but it might take away some of the gnawing in their stomachs. Yesterday they had managed to knock a couple of small birds from the trees but today they hadn't found anything. To make things worse, it had rained most of the day.

In the distance she could still hear the sound of the water tumbling over the falls they had passed at midday. She remembered those falls from the time she went to the coast with her mother. They had to climb the trail to get around them back then. There was still a long way to go but soon they would be in the part of the Great River where the Buggishaman had settled.

They drank the bark water and each took a piece of the softened bark to chew while they walked. Shanawdithit doused the fire and Doodlebewshet helped Linguitt to her feet.

"I don't want to go any farther, Mother."

"You have to Linguitt. We can't stay here."

"Why not Mother? My feet hurt. I'm too sick."

"There is nothing here for us dear. We don't have any food. We need to get to the coast. There will be food there."

"How do you know?"

"Your father has been there many times and brought back food. I have been there before as well. It will be alright. Just follow Shanawdithit."

"Why should I follow her? Who put her in charge? She's not your real daughter. I am," she replied angrily.

"Don't say things like that, Linguitt. She has been a good sister to you."

"I don't care," mumbled Linguitt. "Why did I have to be the one to get sick? I lived in the same mamateek, drank the same water and ate the same food as her. Why, Mother?"

"I don't know, Linguitt. Watch your step there."

They slowly continued down the river path toward the coast.

Two hours later the rain finally stopped. Overhead the sky was still thick with cloud, blocking any sunlight that might have found its way through. Their wet, soggy clothes clung to their shivering bodies and their moccasins squelched water with every step. Shanawdithit knew this was not good for Linguitt and they would soon have to stop and make a fire to dry her clothes and warm her up. She glanced back along the trail to make sure Doodlebewshet and Linguitt were still coming. As she turned back she heard a rustling in the bushes just off the path. Squatting to peer through the short evergreens, she saw a rabbit struggling to free itself from a wire noose that was firmly holding it to a small tree. This was a Buggishaman snare. She had heard it described before. Looking back up the path at her two struggling companions she shouted, "Rabbit," and pushed her way through the trees.

She grabbed the squirming animal and quickly dispensed it with her knife. Standing up to make her way back to the path, she held the rabbit up to show the two women and froze.

There on the path, with a gun leveled at her, was a Buggishaman. Staring down that long barrel, she held her breath, waiting for it to spit the fire that would take her life. Slowly she pulled her eyes away from it and looked into the eyes of the Buggishaman. She had seen him before. He had been there that day at the Great Lake when her father and uncle were shot.

Chapter 14
1823

William had left Mary with their five boys and four girls on Barr'd Island about a week ago. He had been home a little over a week this time and that was more than enough. It wasn't that he didn't like being home with the family, but he was easily bored and needed to be doing something. Besides, that house was full of youngsters and every time he turned around he was tripping over one of them. Mary might be able to handle that but he couldn't for long. So much noise got on his nerves.

He took a small party of men and sailed his schooner into the Bay of Exploits where he planned to set fur traps along the Exploits River. It was late April but there were still ice pans bobbing in the swell along the shore. On the way up they had navigated around a large iceberg that had grounded at the mouth of the bay. Inside the bay was littered with smaller pieces of ice that had broken free as the berg slowly foundered in the constantly rolling waves. With all the ice around, the air had a bitter chill about it that the wind tried its best to thrust inside even the heartiest winter coat. Leaning on the rail, he pulled his collar a little tighter around his neck as he watched his men lower the small dory into the cold, clear water. He would be sixty-three this year and he had been at this for forty years. This island of Newfoundland was his home and he loved it, although he often wondered aloud to Mary why they had stayed on Barr'd Island. It was just a barren rock sitting on the edge of the Atlantic Ocean, swept by every storm the sea could fling at it. Of course he wasn't home all that much. Most of his time had been spent on the schooner or roaming the interior around both Gander and Exploits River. He knew this area like the back of his hand.

This place was rugged and isolated but it gave back plenty if you were willing to work at it. He'd fished and trapped this country since he was a teenager. He raised his eyes from the water to the tree laden hills that gently sloped down to the shoreline. The only sign that anyone had been there were the dried cutovers marking the area where he had been harvesting wood over the past year. There was always opportunity to make money here, and he had dabbled in it all.

The only real problem with this place was those Red Indians, he thought. You had to watch yourself when in the country around here. They could sneak up on you and you never knew if they were going to shoot at you or not. Didn't seem to be many of them around now though, not like it was first when he came here. He guessed they had all died off or moved deep into the interior, away from the coast. The crowd up in St. John's wanted to civilize them, but he knew that was never going to work. But if they were willing to pay, he was willing to earn. Truth be known, he'd actually done alright by the Beothuk over the years. They'd provided him with a decent income from time to time. Lord knows he'd needed it with all the mouths he had to feed back on Barr'd Island.

He thought about the time back in 1803 when he'd captured that old Beothuk women in Gander Bay. Afterwards, he'd taken her up to St. John's and they'd paid him fifty pounds for it. Then they'd turned around and sent her back with him along with a load of presents. He had been told to leave the gifts in the interior with her in the hopes of establishing a better relationship with the Beothuk. Another one of their crazy ideas, he'd thought at the time, but their money was good so he brought her back. She had stayed at their house with Mary for almost a year before he had gotten around to taking her back to Gander River. The little that remained of the presents went with her when he left her on the riverbank. She had been reluctant to go and Mary had wanted her to stay. That was before any of the kids had arrived and she had been great company for Mary, but he had his orders and he didn't want to jeopardize any future dealings with the St. John's crowd. Ten days later he returned to the spot where he had left her but there was no sign of her or the presents. Waste leaving those presents there, he figured, because she'd most likely been killed by her own people. Rumours were the Beothuk sacrificed any of their people that had extended contact with white men and he figured that was probably true.

A few years later in 1809 he was hired by Governor John Holloway to lead a winter expedition into the interior of the island in an attempt to make contact with the Beothuk. That had worked out well for him because there wasn't much doing in the winter time anyway and this was a good-paying, easy job. Good thing he had left the old woman on the riverbank or he probably would never have gotten the job, he thought.

He had hired six settlers from the Notre Dame Bay area and two Micmac Indian guides. They had hiked up the frozen Exploits River about sixty miles or so in four days. The weather was good and the river ice was solid, making for good travel. Although there was lots of evidence the Beothuks were around, they didn't make contact with any of them. He figured the Indians had seen them coming and went into hiding. The two they happened to catch a glimpse of disappeared into the woods and didn't show themselves again.

Anyway, the sighting had been enough for him to turn the group around and head back down the river to the coast. He didn't want to take the chance of an ambush now that the Beothuk had been warned. There was no point in risking that. The money wasn't that good.

The following year he had been sought out by the new Governor Duckworth to act as chief guide to Lieutenant David Buchan who was undertaking a new expedition into the interior to establish contact with the Beothuk. That had been an ambitious expedition but it failed just like all the rest. The first time he met Buchan he knew he was a man with a mission and was not the type to accept failure lightly. He quickly learned Buchan ran a tight ship and liked things under his control. They had gone farther up the Exploits River that time, all the way to Red Indian

Lake. There they had surprised a group of Beothuk and actually spent some time with them. The most memorable was their chief, Nonosabasut, whose face was split with a deep red battle scar. He was one of the biggest Indians he'd ever seen. Not the kind of guy you would want to meet on the trail late at night, or even in broad daylight for that matter.

Things had gone pretty good for a while. They had shared a meal with the Indians and given them presents. Buchan and Nonosabasut were getting along great and it seemed there might be a chance but, just like always, the unpredictable Beothuk ruined it for themselves.

William shook his head as he remembered how discouraged Buchan became when they found the headless bodies of Butler and Bouthland at the abandoned camp. He had moped around like some kid who had lost his dog or something.

Even though most of the group consisted of heavily armed soldiers, he had been successful in convincing Buchan of the wisdom of retreating back to the safety of the coast.

That was twelve years ago and he hadn't seen many Indians since. The scattered one he'd caught a glimpse of vanished into the shadows of the woods as soon as they saw him. It was obvious they had no intention of having any contact with the settlers. It was just as well because there was no civilizing them anyhow.

A shout came from the boat below, breaking his train of thought.

"Hey, Mr. Cull. We're ready down here."

Three of the men were sitting in the dory, the youngest, his nephew, was still in the schooner. He would stay aboard until they returned. His job was to make sure the boat stayed safely at anchor. The schooner was a shallow design and didn't draw much water so she could be anchored close to shore, but there was always the chance the wind could come up and push her on the rocks. Someone needed to be there to take care of her.

He turned away from the rail and looked at the young boy.

"You going to be alright here, Tommy?"

"Sure, Uncle Bill!" he replied enthusiastically. "I'll be fine."

"We'll be gone three or four days, maybe even a week. Don't catch the ship afire or anything while I'm gone, and don't go letting anybody aboard that you don't know."

"I'll be careful," Tom replied, trying his best not to show his pride at being left in charge. His wide grin wasn't helping him much.

"You don't have to worry about the Red Indians around here. They won't show their face if they know you are around. I'm not sure there are any of them left anyway."

"I'm alright. I've always got the gun there in the cabin if I need it."

William smiled, "Ok then Tommy. You're the captain while I'm gone." He gave him a mock salute, turned, and clambered down the side of the schooner to the waiting dory.

They pushed off and began to row the dory into the mouth of the river. With the spring runoff the river overflowed its banks in spots and the resulting current pushed back at the boat, forcing the two rowers to strain their backs just to keep the dory moving upstream. By the time they reached the makeshift pier their muscles were aching and they were soaked with sweat.

They landed there, pulled the dory out of the water onto the rocky beach, and unloaded it.

William left two of the men there to continue cutting wood that he would take back with them and sell to Slades. He and Henry continued up river.

As they traveled along the river bank, they set traps for rabbit and fox. Their furs would yield a good return when he took them to St. John's later in the summer, especially the fox. It was said it was all the craze for the high society women these days.

The Exploits River was still a good area for harvesting furs. It hadn't changed much since he had first trapped there some thirty years ago. There were a few more camps set up by the salmon fishermen that weren't occupied this early in the year and there were a lot less of the Red Indians around, but apart from that the land was much the way it had always been. It was a beautiful and peaceful place. After all these years I can finally appreciate how beautiful it really is, he thought. I must be getting old.

They set all their traps by mid-afternoon and made their way back down-river to one of the salmon fishing huts. William had picked it on their way upriver. It had been rebuilt but it was on the same spot as the hut George Rowsell had once owned. He had spent the night there with George years ago on one of his trapping trips up the river. It had been a few years after George's brother, Thomas, was killed by the Beothuk. He remembered sitting on the bunk listening to George tell the story as he gently rocked back and forth in the old rickety rocker. George was pretty upset about it all but he actually made excuses for the Red Indians. He'd said Thomas had been going around shooting the Indians whenever he got a chance and he'd warned him so many times that it would catch up with him someday.

He knew he wouldn't have been as understanding as George if it had been his brother, whether he was shooting the Indians or not.

At dawn William and Henry left the little hut and began to work their way along the trap-line. It was pouring rain all morning and made for a miserable day. Getting off the trail to check the traps meant navigating around the bigger trees to avoid getting a cold shower. The heavily laden branches would happily shed themselves of unwanted water and douse any unlucky traveler who disturbed them. Still, an hour into it, they had half a dozen rabbits and a couple of red fox.

"They'll look good hanging around some woman's neck, William," said Henry as he dangled the two fox from his hand. "Are you getting one for Mary?"

"Where do ya think she's going to wear something like that? Tis only women down there in New York and those Red Indians wear them foxes. Mary would probably smack me up the side of the head if I brought her that."

"Probably would," laughed Henry.

"Listen Henry. There's only about another hour's worth of traps upriver, so why don't you get to work cleaning those animals and I'll dodge on up the line and check out the rest of the snares."

"Alright, Skipper. Looks like the rain is starting to hold up," replied Henry looking up at the overcast sky.

"Looks that way. I'll be back in a couple of hours," said William as he picked up his gun and set out following the path upriver.

The morning's rain had made the path muddy and wet and he had to watch his step on the slippery ground. Lingering patches of snow smeared white streaks over the otherwise brown and black earth. It was a dreary day and he knew it was going to take a while before his soaked clothes would dry off in this weather. The material was cold on his skin and he kept up a brisk walk to stay warm. Maybe it was time to stop traipsing around the country and do something closer to home, he thought, but there is an awful big crowd at home. Maybe that isn't such a great idea.

The first two traps he checked were empty but he could see the one he was approaching had been tripped. A large red fox was held by one of its hind legs. As he got nearer it bared its teeth and snarled at him then turned and frantically ran until the chain holding the trap ran out and jerked it off its feet with a painful yelp.

William quickened his step for fear it would tear itself loose. Holding the barrel of the gun, he clubbed the animal and it dropped to the ground on its side. This one is a beauty, he thought. It will make one of those high society girls in New York very happy to have that draped around her neck.

He thought he heard someone cough so he looked around. There was no one. He was alone. Turning back to the fox, he checked it to make sure it was no longer breathing, opened the trap, and pulled it free. He reset the trap, brushed the ground with a spruce bough to remove any sign he was there, and draped the fox over his shoulder. Standing to his feet, he heard the sound again.

It was clearer this time. There was someone nearby, farther up the path. He checked to make sure the gun was loaded and crept silently along the trail, trying his best to only step on the rocks and grass. He knew the sound of his boots being sucked into the mud would give him away.

Quietly following the river path, he rounded a sharp bend and saw the source of the noise. Two Red Indian women were sitting on the side of the path. The older one had an arm protectively around the younger, who was resting her head in her lap. The young one was the one doing the coughing. As he took a step forward he saw movement from the corner of his eye. Just off the path was a third one standing over one of his snares with a rabbit dangling from her hand.

His first thought was to shoot the thieving Red Indian so he lifted the gun to his shoulder. She let the rabbit slip through her fingers and backed up two steps until a birch tree stopped her in her tracks. She glanced at the other two and looked about wildly.

They were in a stand of birch and alder trees with only the occasional evergreen. It was early spring and the trees had not yet received their covering of leaves. There was nowhere to hide. If this were a month from now she would have easily disappeared, hidden by the covering of leaves. She looked back at the Buggishaman, uncertain what to do. She might be able to outrun him, but what about Doodlebewshet and Linguitt? What chance did they have?

William watched her over the barrel of his gun. She looked like a frightened animal. She was going to run; he could see it in her eyes and in the way she was desperately checking the woods around her. That wouldn't be good. She looked like the healthiest of the three, skinny as she was. She might be the only one that would make it back with him to get his bounty. The other two looked pretty sick, especially the youngest one. He had no desire to chase her through the woods and she looked a lot younger and spryer than him. That was a race he wouldn't win. He needed to convince her that she was in no danger. They weren't carrying any weapons, save for the knives at their side, so there was no real threat here. He lowered the gun and placed it on the ground.

She watched him with those dark, black eyes. He thought she seemed to relax a little but it was hard to tell.

Trying not to make any sudden movements, he opened his bag and pulled out a chunk of one of Mary's partridgeberry cakes. He held it out to her.

Shanawdithit stared at the cake. She could see the purple berries spotted throughout and her mouth filled with saliva. Her world suddenly shrunk to the space between her and the Buggishaman. She needed food, they all did. He was offering food when just a moment ago she was staring down the barrel of his gun. Tentatively, she picked her way through the low brush, closing the distance between them. She reached for the cake, grabbed it from his hand, and ran to Doodlebewshet and Linguitt. Kneeling on the muddy ground, she broke off a piece for each of them. Then she pushed a large piece into her mouth and chewed.

It was nothing like she had ever tasted before. The tang of the berries balanced the sweetness of the cake. She rolled it around in her mouth, savoring the taste, not wanting to swallow and lose it. It was so good, and it was real food. She took another bite and gave the rest to Doodlebewshet and Linguitt.

A tear trickled down her cheek as she watched her two companions enjoying the offering of the Buggishaman. Could it be that they were saved? And by one of the Buggishaman who had killed her father. Last night she had prepared herself for the worse. She knew the disease was getting the best of them and it would be just a matter of time. And now this. There was still a chance. The Buggishaman hadn't killed them. He wouldn't have fed them if he was going to do that. That would make no sense. Her heart was beginning to fill with hope and she didn't have the energy to stop it. Maybe we can make it, she thought, as the tiny ray of light seemed to grow inside her.

William's mind was calculating. He could stay and gather more furs or pack up and take the three Beothuk women to Magistrate Peyton over at Exploits. The Governor will pay a good bounty for three, he thought. It should pay much better than what I stand to get from the furs and I could always come back after delivering them to Exploits. All I need to do is get them to Peyton. I'll get my payment and he can handle it from there. It looks like the young one may not last much longer. I'd better get some food in them and get back to the boat.

The silence was broken with the violent coughing of the young one as she was hit with another spasm.

His mind was made up. If he didn't get them delivered soon he stood to lose that one and he would only get paid for two.

He walked to the snare and pulled it loose from the trees. He retrieved the rabbit that the Beothuk girl had dropped and returned to the path. There were only two more traps set beyond this one. They were most likely empty or the Red Indians would have taken the animals, he reasoned. He decided to leave them. He would pick them up when he returned from Exploits.

Picking up his gun, he motioned for the three to follow him and then he started back the way he came. He took a few steps, stopped, turned around, and waited.

"We must go with him," said Shanawdithit.

"Do you think it is safe?" asked Doodlebewshet.

"Safe from what? What choice do we have? If we don't go, he might shoot us and if not, we will starve. Wherever he is going there will be food."

"Do you think they have medicine to help Linguitt?"

"Probably. It is their disease."

"Alright then, let's go and find out."

Shanawdithit helped her raise Linguitt to her feet and they shuffled down the muddy path behind the Buggishaman.

It was cold and the rain had penetrated their thin cloaks. Shanawdithit shivered as she watched the back of the Buggishaman ahead of her. She wondered what life would be like from here. There was no going back now; that she knew with a certainty.

Henry looked up in surprise from the skin he was scraping. What had William gotten himself into this time? There he was, hiking down the path with three Beothuk following him like dogs on a leash. How had he managed that? he wondered.

Henry pushed to his feet and stood waiting for William to reach him.

"What have you got yourself this time, Bill?"

"Found these three up at the end of our trap-line."

"Looks like they are starving to death."

"Looks that way. I gave them some of Mary's partridge berry cake and they devoured it like they hadn't had a bite in weeks."

"They probably haven't. What are you planning to do with them?"

"Drop them off to Peyton on Exploits Island and claim the bounty, that's what."

"Proves there's still some of them left out there though, doesn't it?"

"Sure does, but by the shape these three are in, I wouldn't say there's many more."

"Listen to that cough. Sounds like she's got consumption. Best stay clear of her."

"That stuff can be pretty contagious."

"They say it's killed a lot of the Indians."

"Let's cook a couple of those rabbit carcasses and feed them. We'll camp here and get back to the boat tomorrow."

"They are looking at them like they would eat them raw," muttered Henry as he tossed the rabbits in a pot and hung it over the fire he had started earlier in the day.

Shanawdithit and her two companions looked on hungrily.

Early the next morning they arrived at the coast where Sid and Wallace were cutting wood. The men were already working on the hillside when Cull and his small party reached the wharf. They had cleared a channel down the side of the hill and were sliding the logs down the steep incline, which ended in a sharp cliff. The logs were shooting over the edge and dropping into the water below, where they were contained in a boom they had strung across the cove. Once they were finished cutting the plan was to tow the boom across the bay to Slade's depot.

William waved and got Sid's attention, signaling for him to join them on the wharf.

Sid nodded and then buried his axe in the trunk of the tree he was stripping of its limbs. He tugged the handkerchief that was dangling from his back pocket, wiped the sweat off his forehead and then began to make his way down the steep hillside.

Approaching the wharf where they were all standing he yelled in his deep booming voice, "So what's all this now, Mr. Cull? What have you got there? Some of them Red Indians," he answered himself.

Sid's voice always threw everyone off, even those who knew him. He stood no more than five foot two yet his deep voice suited someone six or seven feet tall. No one could figure where it came from.

"Looks pretty scrawny, don't they?" he continued. "Where did ya git them to?"

"Yeah Sid, we found them up at the end of our trap-line. I'm taking them over to Exploits to Magistrate Peyton. Are you and Wallace ok here until we get back?"

"We're alright here, Mr. Cull," Sid boomed. "Just leave us some food and we'll be fine. We should have a good load of wood by the time you get back."

"I figure it will take us two, maybe three, days to get up there and back. I'll leave you enough for a week just in case we run into weather or something."

"That will be fine, sir. Wallace will do the cooking. I've never been much good at that, and I suspect he wouldn't eat anything I cooked anyway," he laughed his booming laugh, which more than matched his speaking voice.

"I'll send Tommy ashore with your supplies and then we'll get underway."

They launched the dory and helped the three nervous women climb in. William and Henry joined them and showed them where to sit on the floor. Sid pushed the boat away from the shore and Henry shipped the oars and rowed them out to the waiting schooner.

Arriving at the side of the larger boat, Doodlebewshet anxiously peered up at the deck above them and the wet flimsy rope ladder hanging over the side.

"I'm not climbing that!" she announced.

"Looks like it is the only way up there," Shanawdithit replied from the back of the dory. "You can't stay here in this little boat."

"I'm not getting on that!" she said, vigorously shaking her head as she shrank down in the front of the boat next to Linguitt.

Shanawdithit watched as Cull climbed the short ladder and swung himself onto the deck. It didn't look all that hard, she concluded.

Henry held the dory against the schooner and motioned for the women to follow Cull up the ladder.

Shanawdithit moved to the front of the dory and helped Linguitt to her feet. She was seized with a coughing fit that doubled her over and Shanawdithit had to wait until it subsided to show her where to put her feet on the rope steps. Tommy, who had been standing on the deck watching them since they arrived at the wharf, leaned out over the side, gripped one of Linguitt's hands, and pulled, while Shanawdithit pushed her from behind. When they had safely pulled her onto the deck, Shanawdithit turned back to Doodlebewshet, who was huddled in the front of the dory. She could see the terror in the old woman's eyes.

"It's not that hard. You can do it. I will help you and keep you from falling, just like I did with Linguitt."

"I can't," she whimpered, trying to shrink herself farther into the corner.

"Linguitt is already up there. You must go with her. She needs you to be with her."

Doodlebewshet looked skeptically at the rope and then at the two men grinning down at her from the deck. She looked at the dark water underneath the ladder and then at Shanawdithit. Swallowing hard, she gripped both sides of the rocking boat and slowly pulled herself to her unsteady feet. Her eyes were almost completely closed and she softly moaned in fear.

Henry pulled the dory along the side of the schooner until the ladder was next to where Doodlebewshet crouched in the front.

Shanawdithit reached out, pried Doodlebewshet's fingers loose from the side, and guided her hand to the rope ladder. "Look up. Don't look down," she instructed her.

She forced the fingers of her other hand loose and thrust it towards Tommy, who gripped it and pulled the screaming Doodlebewshet up and over the side.

Shanawdithit scrambled up the ladder to find Doodlebewshet collapsed in a heap and weeping on the deck. The Buggishaman were standing there laughing at her.

"Put them down in the cabin, Tommy," said William. "Then I need you to carry some supplies in to Sid and Wallace before we get underway."

"We're leavin' then are we, Uncle Bill?"

"Yes. Sid and Wallace are staying here while we take those three up to Exploits. Oh and don't get too close to that one," he said, pointing at Linguitt. "I think she has consumption, and you don't want to catch that."

By midafternoon they were underway and the wharf soon disappeared behind them as they sailed around the grounded iceberg and out into the open waters of the bay. The Beothuks were below deck in the cabin and Henry and Tommy, who were manning the sails, had pulled on heavier coats. William stood in the wheelhouse steering the schooner around the random pieces of drift ice. As they moved farther offshore it thinned out and it was no longer necessary to run the zig zag course, so they made much better time.

William wanted to get as far out the bay as possible before nightfall. Once the evening came they would have to drop anchor. With all this ice it was too risky to sail in the dark. He couldn't afford to damage this schooner. Of course, what he could and couldn't afford would soon change once he sold the three Indians.

Shanawdithit sat on the edge of one of the bunks with her hands braced on the edge and her head bowed. She was fighting the nausea that washed over her as the boat rolled and pitched on the water. Linguitt had fallen into a restless sleep on the floor and Doodlebewshet sat next to her with her back against the edge of the other bunk. None of them had been enclosed in a boat like this before and their stomachs could not accept the unpredictable movement. The younger Buggishaman had left them a bucket and it was getting regular use. The rancid smell coming from its contents made the air heavy and almost unbreathable. The tiny room had two small closed windows in addition to the hatch where they had entered. There wasn't enough headroom to completely stand erect without bumping the ceiling. Not being able to feel the air on her face was making it much harder. Being confined in this small space was becoming unbearable.

She had no idea what the Buggishaman planned to do with them, but right now it didn't matter. Maybe death was better than feeling like this.

The light coming through the window had turned gray and the inside of the room was now filled with shadows. Night was wrapping itself around the tossing boat and when she peered out the window through the deepening gloom it seemed the shoreline was closer than it had been before. The tossing and rolling of the boat had all but stopped. She could hear the Buggishaman outside shouting to each other. Maybe they were stopping for the night.

The hatch slid up and the face of the young Buggishaman appeared in the opening. The rush of cold air washed over her face and she lifted her head and drew in a deep breath. The Buggishaman waved to her to come outside and she scrambled up the few steps from the cabin. Once on deck she could see they were no longer moving. The shoreline was close and she looked at it longingly. The crisp salty air was clearing her head and she was feeling better already.

Turning back, she reached down her hand and helped Doodlebewshet as she pushed whimpering Linguitt up the cabin steps. She was still coughing but Shanawdithit could see the outside air was already helping to revive her. They wouldn't be going back down there, she decided.

Doodlebewshet and Linguitt sat on the deck with their backs propped against the raised hatch in the middle of the boat. Shanawdithit stood at the low rail, gazing at the nearby shoreline. She folded her arms around herself against the chilly wind. She became aware of someone standing close behind her and turned. The young Buggishaman was standing there with a blanket in his hand. He extended it toward her and she took it gratefully, offering him a tentative smile. He then brought blankets to the other two women and went below again. Moments later he emerged from the cabin with the bucket. He tied a line around the handle and tossed it over the side.

"It's foul down there, Uncle Bill," he exclaimed. "They sure ain't got their sea legs," he laughed.

"Probably never in a boat before," muttered William. "They'll want to sleep up here I expect. I don't think they will want to go back down there."

"One of us will have to stay awake and watch them," said Henry, who was busy cooking the rabbits he had skinned. "We have no idea what they might do when we are asleep."

"These three!" exclaimed Tommy. "What do you think they could do?"

"They could kill you in your sleep, boy," replied William harshly. "They are not as tame as they look. Don't you go and start trusting Red Indians. They've always been killing us settlers. You know what they do when they kill you Tommy? They cut your head off, that's what. I saw it up at Red Indian

Lake with Lieutenant Buchan. You don't want to find your head stuck up on a pole now, do you?"

Tommy looked from his uncle to the Red Indians and swallowed nervously.

Henry kept his head bowed over the cooking pot. He had heard the stories of the expedition to Red Indian Lake many times before. He knew William was trying to scare young Tommy but he also knew there was always a chance these Red Indians would turn on them. They must feel trapped on this boat and they have no idea what is going to happen to them. He knew he would sleep far away from them with one eye open.

"I will take the first shift and wake you when it is your turn, Henry," announced William.

Henry began spooning out portions of the stew he had prepared and placed bowls in front of the Indians.

"Probably not going to keep any of this down anyway. Waste of a good stew," he muttered as he returned to the stove and dished up servings for the rest of them.

"Break off some of that bread and give them," he instructed Tommy.

Tommy did as he was told, but this time he approached the women a little more cautiously. The one at the rail was talking to the older one in that strange language of theirs. Tommy wondered how anyone could make any sense out of those sounds they were making.

"How is she doing, Doodlebewshet?"

"She's very sick, Shanawdithit. I don't know what to do for her," replied the older woman as a tear slowly coursed down her leathery cheek. "I think she may die from this."

"Let's wake her and try and get her to eat something," said Shanawdithit as she knelt on the wooden deck next to them.

She dipped the bread in the warm broth and placed it on Linguitt's lips. She opened her eyes and looked at Shanawdithit dazedly as the salty liquid dribbled down her throat. Weakly, she reached for the dripping bread and stuffed it in her mouth. Shanawdithit smiled at her reassuringly and pushed the bowl toward her.

Tommy couldn't sleep. He paced the deck restlessly thinking about what his uncle had said. The full moon overhead watched him intently as he walked around the deck of the small boat, completing circuit after circuit. He was careful to keep the three Red Indians in his sight at all times.

He hadn't thought there was any danger from these three until his uncle had reminded him about the Red Indian Lake incident. Now he was not so sure. They sure didn't look dangerous. The young one looked more like she was dying. The one who had been standing at the rail looked stronger. Maybe she was the dangerous one. Perhaps she had a knife hidden in her cloak. His hand involuntarily rubbed his throat as he walked by the blanket-wrapped women again. But he had seen no anger in her eyes when he had given her the blanket, only gratitude. He shook his head in confusion and continued walking.

"Better get some sleep, boy," said his uncle as he passed him standing outside the wheelhouse.

"Soon," he muttered as he continued down the other side of the schooner, passing through the small cloud of tobacco smoke from William's glowing cigarette. He noticed the older one had cradled the younger one in her lap. The stronger one lay on the deck asleep. He had made it halfway up the other side of the deck when the singing stopped him. It was coming from the older woman who was singing softly to the young one. The sound was hauntingly lonely. He stared across the moonlit deck at them. Although he was scared of them, he felt a little sad at the shadowy picture there before him. He knew if the stories he had heard were right he was probably looking at some of the few remaining Red Indians, maybe even the last of them. He knew that melancholy sound and forlorn picture would stick with him the rest of his life. With a small involuntary shiver, he tore his eyes away, walked back to the wheelhouse, nodded to his uncle, and went inside to sleep.

Chapter 15
1823

Standing on the wharf, he watched the schooner lower its sails and make its way around the point and into the shelter of the protected harbour. He recognized it as William Cull's boat and as it drew nearer he could see him standing at the wheelhouse. What was even more interesting was the three figures standing at the front of the boat. It appeared to be three Beothuk.

John had known William Cull for years. He had worked on the larger rivers trapping for furs for John's father for some time when John had first come to this colony. Cull had been with them on the Exploits River in 1819 when the Red Indian Demasduit was captured. They had shared a somewhat guarded relationship since that day. The killing of the second Indian had not been reported and it remained a secret amongst the men who were there. John wasn't sure who had fired that shot; it may have been Cull. He really was not sure. Regardless, the subject remained off limits and they never talked about it after the trial.

He held up his hand to greet Cull, who was steering the boat into its berth.

"Where did you find those?" he shouted up to Cull once the boat had docked.

"Up near the head of the Exploits River. They were raiding my traps," William answered as he strode down the plank from the deck of the schooner.

"Looks in bad shape. How long have you had them?"

"Couple of days. They were pretty sick on the boat. Wouldn't stay below in the cabin. First time on a boat I would think. It sounds like the young one has the makings of consumption, and maybe the older onc too. We tried to keep away from them as much as we could."

"Have they eaten anything?"

"Some. We fed them before they got on the boat. They ate like they hadn't seen food in a while. Looks like they didn't keep much of it down though. Not very good sailors, I'm afraid," He chuckled.

"Hey Tommy, help them down the plank, will ya," he shouted up to the boat.

Without getting too close, Tommy motioned to the Red Indians to use the plank to get off the boat.

Shanawdithit went first, followed by Doodlebewshet, who was guiding Linguitt down the narrow plank that swayed with the gentle rocking of the boat.

"What's your plan, William?" asked Peyton as he watched the old woman step onto the wharf and collapse to her knees in relief.

"I brought them here for the bounty. There's no other reason to have come all the way out here. You pay up and I'll be on my way, John."

"What's the hurry?"

"I left a couple of men back at the river and I need to get back to them."

"Follow me up to the store then and I will settle up with you."

"Bounty is more for three, right?"

Peyton didn't answer as he turned to the Red Indians and motioned them to follow him.

He had decided he would find a place for them to sleep in one of his empty store rooms until he could take them up to St. John's. If it was consumption they had, he didn't want to expose anyone to that. They would be there under his care for a month or so. There was too much drift ice along the coast to make the trip this early. He would take them later in June when the weather was better. Anyway, the Indians would need some time to get on their feet before taking another boat trip. They looked like they were starving to death.

Standing on the wharf, the first thing Shanawdithit noticed was that it wasn't moving under her feet, even though she could hear the waves lapping against its sides. A slow smile crept across her face as she released a breath she had been unknowingly holding. She was off the boat. She had never before felt a sickness like that; one that completely drains you from the inside out, leaving you longing for death to relieve you from the misery.

Standing there she still felt weak and her stomach was still churning a little, but the feel of solid ground under her feet and the cool wind on her face was reviving her surprisingly fast.

She looked around the harbour. There were more wooden houses here than she had ever seen. Some were bigger than others, some taller. They were sprinkled around the harbour, mostly all on higher ground back from the water. Along the shoreline a number of wharves jutted out into the water with boats of all sizes tied up to them. At the nearest one a Buggishaman was tossing fish from his boat up onto the wharf where several more were cutting the fish and dropping them into a barrel. Seabirds were swooping to grab the discarded insides, shrieking and fighting one another for each scrap. The wharf they were standing on was much bigger than the others. Crates were being unloaded from another boat tied up next to the one they had arrived in. At the end of the wharf, where it met the shoreline, stood several larger wooden buildings. Her eye was drawn to a bunch of clothes wildly flapping in the wind. They were hung on a line strung between a tree and a house that was sitting on the hill just above them. This was a very noisy and busy place.

Above the conversation between the Buggishaman that brought them on the boat and the one that had been standing on the wharf, she heard the cries of children at play. It had been a long time since she heard that. It reminded her of home when she was younger and living at the Great Lake. Those had been happier times.

She had no idea where they were but it had taken two days to get here, so she knew they were a long way from home. With a sinking feeling in her heart she knew she would never see home again. The Buggishaman seemed to have other plans for them. She wondered which direction led home as she looked up at the gray clouds scampering across the sky.

She looked back at the boat. The one they called Tommy was standing on the deck watching her. He had seemed nice at first but later he kept his distance as if he were scared of her. She wondered what had happened. She didn't remember doing anything that might have threatened him.

So far the Buggishaman were treating them well. There didn't seem to be any danger here. She wished she could understand what they were saying, but they were talking in that funny language. She hoped they were done with the boat. She never wanted to set foot on it again.

The Buggishaman from the wharf waved for them to follow him as he began to walk toward the buildings. Shanawdithit gripped Linguitt's arm and helped her stand up from where she had been sitting on the wharf. She seemed to be a little better and wasn't coughing as much as before. Maybe the air was doing her good. Perhaps this place would be better for her.

"Where do you think they are taking us, Shanawdithit?" asked Linguitt.

"To those buildings, I think."

"At least we will get out of this damp, chilly air," exclaimed Doodlebewshet. "It will be nice to get some shelter and maybe something to eat," she mumbled as she shuffled along several steps behind the two girls. As she walked she kneaded her side with her hand to relieve the ache. This had been a long, tough trip and the cramps and pain in her body reminded her that she was an old woman. She hoped this was the end of it. She knew that what she was feeling inside was the beginning of the Buggishaman's coughing disease that was consuming her daughter. Watching the two girls, she tried to push aside the sense of dread that settled over her like a heavy blanket. Her daughter needed her more than ever. It was more important she be there for Linguitt than worrying about her own sickness.

The Buggishaman from the wharf had reached one of the smaller buildings and stood there holding the tall wooden door open. He glanced back at the Indians and then entered. Shanawdithit and the others followed him inside.

They were standing on the rough wooden floor of a storeroom. There were wide shelves running around the sides and the far end. Most of the shelves were empty except for a few ropes and nets. Toward the back a ladder led up to a loft that appeared to be filled with dry grass. Shanawdithit realized that was where the strong smell was coming from that filled the whole building. She remembered someone telling a story at the campfire a long time ago about how the Buggishaman cut and dried the grass to feed their animals through the long winter months. The smell was strong but somehow comforting.

The two Buggishaman unrolled some sails and spread them over the lower shelves and covered them with blankets. The Buggishaman indicated that this was to be their sleeping place and then left, closing the door behind them.

Shanawdithit walked to the door and tried lifting the latch after they left. It swung toward her. They weren't prisoners. She opened the door enough to look outside. A small group of children had gathered outside and were watching the door curiously. She smiled at them and closed the door again.

Peyton had waited until June to make the trip up to St. John's. By then the ice had all disappeared, with the exception of a couple of grounded bergs unable to escape the grip of the rocky ocean floor that had snagged them earlier in May. Even they had lost much of their former size and shape as the warming water slowly eroded their surface and inevitably returned them to the water of their birth.

He was on the return trip along the coast with the three Red Indians, along with a large stock of supplies for them to take back to their tribe. At least that was the plan. He had delivered them to Buchan, who was acting for Governor Hamilton in his absence. Buchan, who saw this as another splendid opportunity to establish relations with the declining Beothuk nation, quickly gathered together provisions for the three to take back with them to the Exploits River in the hope they would find their way back to their camp. He had ordered Peyton to return with all haste and deposit them at or near the place where William Cull had found them. Buchan believed they would find their way home from there. He hoped they would convince the others, if there were any others, to return to the coast where they might be helped. Buchan had told Peyton that he was convinced he had reached an understanding with them and this time the plan would work. He had wanted to accompany Peyton but his duties in St. John's wouldn't allow him the time. However, Buchan had impressed on him the importance of his mission and the absolute need for it to succeed. Although Peyton did share

Buchan's belief that something needed to be done to help the Beothuk, he did not share his optimism.

Standing near the rail, Peyton watched the Red Indians thoughtfully. They were sitting on the deck with their backs against the small boat that Buchan had provided for them to make their way upriver. It was lashed securely to the deck with all their provision underneath a tarpaulin inside it. He was not too sure these three had the strength to make it back upriver, but, like Buchan, he thought it was worth a try. The old woman and the youngest were sick and definitely had contracted consumption. They didn't seem to have much strength to go wandering around looking for their tribe. It was unlikely those of their tribe they had left were still at the same camp anyway.

At least its warmer weather now that we are into July, he thought. The three women had flatly refused to spend any time inside the cabin and had slept out on the deck on the trip down as well as now. It had been a tough enough job to coax them back on the boat in the first place; in fact, they had to be forced on for the trip down to St. John's. Coming back wasn't as bad. He didn't know if that was because they were getting more used to the boat or if they thought they were going home. They must have had a really rough trip on the boat with Cull, he thought.

Peyton decided not to stop in at Exploits Island but continued up the Bay of Exploits to the mouth of Charles Brook. He wanted to discharge the Indians as soon as he could. He didn't want either one of them dying on his ship and it didn't seem as if the young one had much life left in her. He landed them ashore with their boat and provisions, and tried his best to make them understand how to get to the mouth of the Exploits River. Then he left them there.

Chapter 16
1823

"Why are they leaving us here?"

"I think Bukn wants us to take all this stuff back to the tribe," Shanawdithit replied. "I think the Buggishaman want to make up for all the things they did to our people."

"Not much chance of that. They already kicked us out. They won't be interested in taking us back for this. Besides we've been gone too long. They are moved by now. We are not able to make the trip back up the Great River."

"I know."

"Well, at least we are off that boat! How are you feeling, Linguitt?"

"I'm sick mother. I don't want to go any farther," she said with tears in her eyes.

Doodlebewshet looked at her sadly. "We will rest for now. Maybe you will feel better tomorrow, now that we are back on land."

"I don't think so," Linguitt sputtered as the coughing started again. "I just want to die and get it over with."

"Don't say things like that. We will be alright. Do you know where we are, Shanawdithit? This is not the Great River," said Doodlebewshet.

"That's why they gave us the boat, I guess. He..." Shanawdithit said while nodding to the disappearing boat out on the bay, "...drew in the sand. The Great River is that way. We have to follow the shoreline."

"Maybe tomorrow. Now we need to find a place to sleep and Linguitt needs to rest. We aren't going any farther today."

"I don't want any more boats," said Linguitt.

"We were treated well by the Buggishaman," said Shanawdithit thoughtfully.

"We ate well with them. Now we are on our own again. What happens when this food runs out? Why did they push us out? Is it because of the sickness?" wondered Doodlebewshet.

"I'm not sure. The Buggishaman do some strange things."

Linguitt lay on the warm sand curled into a tight ball, her body racked with coughing.

"I wonder where Jaywritt and Aaduth are?" thought Doodlebewshet aloud.

Shanawdithit didn't answer. They have been gone too long, she thought. They would have come looking for us if they were alright.

She walked down to the boat, untied the tarpaulin, pulled out several blankets, and brought them up the beach to the other two.

"Here," she said, "we may as well use them. We can sleep here on the beach tonight. Tomorrow we will take the boat up to the Great River and find a good campsite. We can stay there until the food is all gone. Maybe someone from the tribe will come to the coast and find us."

"Maybe, but most likely not."

Shanawdithit spread her blanket on the grass at the edge of the sandy beach. She sat there looking out over the quiet water, listening to the song birds flittering around the trees behind her. She thought of drawing something but she felt too tired. So much had happened in the past few weeks. She knew she had to draw some of it but it would have to be later when they had a campsite. When the Buggishaman Bukn saw the drawing in her pouch he gave her paper and a small wooden stick that marked. She had watched Bukn make marks on the paper as he was talking to her. She wanted to try that but she hadn't had a chance yet. It seemed to be a much easier way to draw than the fire stick she always used.

She lay down on the blanket and stared up at the moon and all the sparkling lights in the sky around it. Some said those lights were the spirits of her ancestors. There are many more lights up there than there are Beothuks down here, she thought. She was wondering where her spirit would one day appear in the sky as she drifted off to sleep.

She was walking on the frozen river with Preduc a few paces ahead of her. The wind was driving the snow in their faces so she kept her head bent low. All she could see through her squinted eyes was her feet. She sensed they should stop but she couldn't get Preduc to hear her above the howling storm. Something bad was going to happen but she couldn't remember what. She had been here before on other nights. It was something about the river, she thought, as she struggled to grasp the memory that lurked just out of reach. Then, with a sharp crack, the ice opened underneath her feet. She was under the ice. Desperately, she clawed at the smooth surface just inches from her face. Cold rushing water was all around her, pulling her along with it. She tried to breathe but found only water to fill her lungs. Just to her left the caribou Preduc had been carrying watched her with dark accusing eyes. As she watched, its lips pulled up over its teeth in a triumphant grin and it turned and swam away under the ice. Frantically, she tried to follow, but her wooden legs would not move. With a cry, she jolted awake gasping for air with the blanket tightly tangled around her legs. Kicking it off, she lay there waiting for her breathing to settle down.

Doodlebewshet and Linguitt were still asleep nearby. While she had been asleep the moon had slipped behind the clouds. The night was very still.

Sleep did not return easily. She did not want to return to that nightmare again. Her ancestors were no longer visible in the dark sky overhead. It was as if everyone had left her and she was all alone. It was much later when she finally fell asleep.

When she opened her eyes, Doodlebewshet and Linguitt were eating from the provisions the Buggishaman had given them. She had slept late.

"Did you have the dream again?" asked Doodlebewshet as she saw Shanawdithit stirring.

"Yes. How did you know?"

"I heard you cry out to him in your sleep."

"I thought I was alone."

Shanawdithit accepted the dried beef Doodlebewshet was holding out to her, bit off a piece, and began to chew.

"Why do I keep having the same dream?"

"He visits you in your sleep. He was taken before he should have been."

"Why are the dreams always so scary?"

"It was a scary way to die, Shanawdithit."

"I wish he were still here."

"He is one of those lights you love to watch up there," she said, pointing at the sky.

Shanawdithit smiled softly and pushed to her feet. She looked past Doodlebewshet into Linguitt's tortured eyes and the smile faded.

"We had better get going," she said.

They climbed into the little boat and Shanawdithit began to row like Peyton had shown her. It was awkward at first, but after several clumsy attempts, she fell into the rhythm and they began to slowly move in a straight line along the heavily wooded coastline. They stayed close to the shore and Doodlebewshet kept an eye out for Buggishaman. Shanawdithit did not want to suffer the fate of her mother. The Buggishaman had treated them well but she knew it would be dangerous to trick herself into believing they were all like that. It was better to be safe, and close enough to escape into the woods if they needed too.

It took two more days to reach the mouth of what they believed was the Great River. Twice they crossed to the other side of the bay under the cover of darkness to bypass small settlements of the Buggishaman. Shanawdithit did most of the rowing. Doodlebewshet was becoming almost as sick as her daughter and no longer had the strength to help much. The only difference was that Doodlebewshet never complained.

Shanawdithit was beginning to feel that all this was pointless. She was probably only taking the other two to find a place to die. They had been around her so much she probably had the disease inside her too.

Her hands were raw from the wooden paddles but she kept rowing through the night while Doodlebewshet and Linguitt slept at the back of the boat. She didn't want to sleep in the dark anyway. There were too many dreams. Last night she had relived that horrible day she watched the Buggishaman murder her mother, and her brother and sister. She began to sing softly to keep her mind off the dream. She imagined what it must have been like before she was born, when this bay would have been dotted with mamateeks and the only people sleeping along the shore would have been Beothuk. She wished she could have seen that. It must have been a happy place then.

They only managed about a half day's journey up the Great River in the boat. By that time, Shanawdithit was exhausted from rowing and the river current was pushing back so hard she was making very little progress anyway. Doodlebewshet sat in the back of the boat and Linguitt lay whimpering in the front, just behind Shanawdithit's seat.

Shanawdithit took a quick glance over her shoulder and saw a small clearing ahead on the right side of the river. She decided this was as far as she was going to row and aimed the boat across the current. Making one last effort against the current, she pulled hard on the paddles until the front of the boat ground into the rocky bottom at the edge of the river. With relief, she swung the paddles into the boat and jumped over the side into the shallow water. Doodlebewshet went into the water on the other side and together they lifted the nose of the boat onto the grass at the edge of the river. Doodlebewshet helped her daughter climb out of the boat while Shanawdithit removed all the provisions.

Shanawdithit stood for a moment in the warm sun, surveying the grassy clearing. It was surrounded by tall birch trees that grew all the way up the gentle slope of the hill behind the clearing. A narrow brook trickled along the treeline on one side until it found its way down to join the larger river. It was an inviting and peaceful place, a place that felt more like home than all the places they had visited in the Buggishaman's world. She looked at Doodlebewshet and the old woman nodded in agreement. They would build a shelter and stay here for a while.

Doodlebewshet loosely looped the boat's line to a tree stump and they began carrying the provisions to the back of the clearing, where they planned to build their shelter. They returned from carrying their final load just in time to see the boat, broken free from its loose tether, drifting down the river. Shanawdithit stood near where Linguitt was sitting on the river bank and watched as the current took it downriver out of sight.

"No harm done," said Linguitt. "We were finished with it anyway."

"I've done enough rowing of those things for a lifetime," laughed Shanawdithit.

Doodlebewshet fondly watched the two girls there at the river's edge. She loved them both. Even though Shanawdithit was not her own she thought of her as a daughter. She had her mother Shanadee's looks but her father's gentle personality. She had experienced more than her share of loss but still carried herself with a quiet strength. She was a good sister to Linguitt.

Linguitt had never been a strong person. Now that she was so sick, she needed someone to lean on. Although her jealousy of Shanawdithit often rose to the surface, she still took the help that Shanawdithit so willingly offered. She seemed to be doing a little better the last few days, thought Doodlebewshet. The medicine the Buggishaman had given them had helped. Her coughing fits did not happen as often and when they did they weren't as bad. Mine, on the other hand, are getting worse, she thought. Maybe I should take some of the liquid as well. But if I do that I'd be taking it away from Linguitt. No, I think I will do without.

When the boat finally disappeared from sight, the girls returned to where Doodlebewshet was sitting. Linguitt flopped on the grass next to her mother. Shanawdithit picked up one of the two shiny hatchets from the provisions and began to chop down small trees to build a shelter for them. At first they thought they would build a mamateek but neither Linguitt nor

Doodlebewshet had the energy to do the work, so they settled for a large lean-to.

"I don't think we should build this near the river path," said Doodlebewshet. "The Buggishaman travels this path regularly."

"Do you think we are still in danger?" asked Linguitt.

"Yes. Just because the Buggishaman we met were friendly doesn't mean they all are. The ones out here wouldn't change that quickly."

"I think we should stay out of their way," agreed Shanawdithit. "It's better to be safe."

"Let's follow that brook and find a more hidden place to build," said Shanawdithit as she picked up a portion of the provisions.

The other two shared out the provisions that remained and followed her into the woods.

They hadn't gone far when they found another small clearing that more than suited their needs. They built the lean-to between two large fir trees and settled in.

For a short time, life was good. They passed the warm summer days resting and doing little more than enjoying each other's company. They saw no one other than the wildlife that shared the woods with them.

Almost a week passed before their food supply exhausted and left them in the same position as when William Cull found them. The medicine had run out before that and the disease was consuming Linguitt once again. The disease had advanced more quickly in Doodlebewshet and she was at the point where she could no longer care for her daughter. Shanawdithit knew with a certainty that neither of them would last much longer here. It was time to leave and try to get help from the Buggishaman. If they didn't leave now they would die here. She had to do what she could to help them. They had no one else.

"Today we leave for the coast," she announced.

Doodlebewshet looked at her weakly and nodded. Shanawdithit saw tears just below the surface, and her heart tightened within her chest. These two were her family; the only family she had left. Doodlebewshet and her Uncle Jaywritt had taken her in and treated her as a daughter when she lost her parents and siblings. Doodlebewshet was like a mother to her and seeing her and Linguitt this way broke her heart. She felt so helpless. There was nothing she could do herself but the Buggishaman had medicine. If she could get them back to the coast maybe they could be saved.

Shanawdithit helped them to their feet and gathered up the clothes, the rest they would leave behind. She then took the lead back through the woods to the river path. A light rain was falling from the gray sky overhead as they emerged from the trees into the larger clearing. Two caribou that had been grazing on the long grass bounded away into the woods. The three watched them longingly and then continued on the path downriver toward the coast.

Travel was painfully slow. Neither of her companions had much strength left and the little that remained was used up by the relentless coughing. She noticed the front of both their cloaks were stained with blood that darkened each time they coughed. She had seen this before and knew it was a sign they were near the end. Although she was filled with a sense of urgency to get to the coast, there was no way she could get them to move any faster. They were moving as fast as they could.

What had taken them a half day in the boat stretched well into a full day on the return trip. By the time they reached the beach at the mouth of the Great River the evening shadows were crowding them on all sides.

Doodlebewshet and Linguitt collapsed on the grass that ran down from the treeline to the edge of the rocky beach. Shanawdithit knew that was as far as they would be going. She covered them with the extra blankets they brought and sat with her knees drawn up, staring out over the bay. She now felt that same feeling that she had that day on the hillside as she watched her family die; empty and afraid. In the trees behind her the songbirds had fallen asleep on their perches. As the last light was smothered by darkness, all was quiet except for the waves gently running up the beach below.

She fell asleep wondering what tomorrow would bring.

Her dreams were interrupted by the shrill screeching of quarrelling seagulls. Pushing to her elbow, she blinked away the sleep and looked to see what all the commotion was about. All along the beach the waves were rolling hundreds of tiny silver fish up on the sand. The gulls were gorging themselves on the bounty wriggling in the froth left behind by the retreating tide. With a shout of delight, she sprang to her feet and raced down to the water's edge. She stood there in the water and watched as the little fish swarmed about her feet and then were swept up on the beach with the breaking wave. Laughing aloud, she grabbed them by the handfuls and ran back to where the other two slept. She dropped them on the grass and ran back for more until she was sure she had more than they could eat.

Doodlebewshet had awaken with all the commotion and had managed to start a fire in the sand. Linguitt still lay sleeping. Doodlebewshet watched her worriedly as she spread the little fish on the rocks they had arranged around the fire.

Within a few minutes the fish were ready and Shanawdithit and Doodlebewshet sat on the damp sand eating their fill while watching whales feasting off the silver fish just offshore. Behind them Linguitt slept on.

After they had eaten all the fish they could stomach, Shanawdithit broke the silence, "I am going to find help. You stay with Linguitt and I will bring them back here."

"I don't think she will last the day," Doodlebewshet replied sadly. "I don't think anyone can help her now."

Shanawdithit wrapped her arms around her adopted mother and held her tight. Together they cried.

She wasn't sure how long they were linked that way but she finally released herself, wiped her eyes, and stood to her feet.

She glanced at the still figure of Linguitt and began to walk along the beach, back toward the settlements they had passed on their way here. "I'll be back as soon as I can," she called over her shoulder. She heard Doodlebewshet mumble something in acknowledgement.

At the end of the cove before she walked around the point, she looked back at the two distant figures on the beach. Doodlebewshet was cradling her daughter and, although she couldn't hear, it seemed she was singing to her. Shanawdithit thought she had never seen a lonelier picture. She brushed a stray tear from her face, turned, and hurried around the point.

She trudged along the shoreline around coves and points until the sun was high overhead. Feeling thirsty, she stopped to drink the cool refreshing water from a trickling brook that meandered its way down the hillside to the beach. When she stood again she spotted smoke rising above the trees in the distance. She began to run. Picking her way around the boulders that formed the rocky point at the end of the cove, she saw the house. It stood alone in the next cove set back from the beach on the edge of the woods. The smoke she had seen was drifting lazily into the sky from a pipe sticking out of the top of the house. The door was standing wide open. In the small yard in front of the house several chicken busily scratched the ground in search of food. She noticed a small boat tied to the wharf. It was empty. She looked past the house at the vegetable garden and saw someone bent over the rows of plants. As she continued running up the beach, a woman walked around the far side of the house with a bucket of water in each hand separated by a large wooden hoop.

She was taller than Shanawdithit and older than Doodlebewshet. Her hair was tied back in a knot behind her head, revealing every weathered line in her gaunt face.

Shanawdithit approached within a few feet of her and they stood there assessing one another. She had carefully set the buckets on the ground and stepped over the wooden hoop.

This close, Shanawdithit could see the Emamoose was head and shoulders over her. The imposing figure made her nervous until she looked into her eyes. There was a kindness there that contradicted the harshness of her rigid, frowning face.

The woman turned and shouted in the direction of the field where Shanawdithit had seen the other Buggishaman. She saw him turn and look in their direction. He quickly scrambled to his feet and hurried toward them. He was carrying a long gun in his hand.

Shanawdithit fell to her knees in front of the Emamoose. She was afraid they would kill her. She heard the Buggishaman run up to them breathing heavily but she was afraid to look up. She knelt there with her head bowed, listening to them talk. The Emamoose was talking the most.

Through the tangle of thick hair that had fallen down over her face, she saw the Emamoose's boot appear in front of her and she felt a hand lightly touch her shoulder. She brushed the hair from her face and looked up. The Emamoose was smiling at her. The Buggishaman was standing to the side with the gun cradled in the crook of his arm. He was looking over her shoulder, searching the beach and the woods surrounding the cove.

The Emamoose picked up a tin that was tied to one of the buckets, dipped it into the water, and offered it to Shanawdithit. She drank the cool, sweet water, wiping the drippings from her chin with her dirty sleeve. Standing to her feet, she handed the empty tin back to the Emamoose.

Shanawdithit pointed back the way she had come and waved for them to follow her. After two steps she stopped and looked back. They hadn't moved. They were just standing there watching her. She had to make them understand somehow. There was no time to waste. She needed to get back to Doodlebewshet and Linguitt. Walking back to the Emamoose, she tentatively reached out, grasped her hand, and tried to pull her. The Buggishaman raised the gun but the Emamoose waved to him to put it down. She shook her head no to Shanawdithit and pulled her hand free.

Desperately, Shanawdithit looked around her. She saw a stick on the ground and rushed to pick it up, startling the hens in her path. Grabbing the short stick, she returned to them and knelt on the ground again. She began to draw in the dirt. When she finished the third stick figure she patted her chest and pointed at it. She pointed to the other two figures and lay on her face in the dirt. Looking up into the Emamoose's eyes, she thought she saw understanding there. Perhaps my drawings will finally pay off, she thought with guarded relief.

The Emamoose began talking excitedly to the Buggishaman, waving her hands around in front of his face. She then turned and pointed along the beach the way Shanawdithit had. Shanawdithit turned and hurried down the beach. She stopped after going a short way and looked back. This time they were following her. She turned and hurried on, glancing behind every now and then to make sure they were still following.

Several times she had to stop and wait for them to catch up but eventually she rounded the final point and saw Doodlebewshet sitting next to Linguitt in the distance. As she got closer, she saw Doodlebewshet had drawn the blanket over her head and was rocking back and forth on the grass. A low heartbreaking moan was coming from under the blanket. She realized it was too late for Linguitt and, with a heavy heart, she quickly covered the remaining distance and knelt on the grass in front of Doodlebewshet. The old woman lifted her head and acknowledged her through tear-filled eyes.

"I brought help," said Shanawdithit, indicating the two approaching along the sandy beach.

"It's too late Shanawdithit. She is already gone," she sobbed and bent over to the ground as the coughing overtook her.

"We must get you to shelter, Doodlebewshet."

"I won't leave my daughter."

"We will bury her first. They will help," said Shanawdithit, nodding toward the Buggishaman and Emamoose who were now standing on the beach behind her. "I will show them."

Doodlebewshet nodded weakly.

"We will take her down to the point," said Shanawdithit, pointing back in the direction they had just come. She motioned to the Buggishaman that he should pick up Linguitt and carry her, then she helped Doodlebewshet stand to her feet. She draped one of Doodlebewshet's arms around her neck, slipped her arm around the old woman's waist, and they began the slow walk to the point. The Buggishaman walked ahead of them with the blanket-covered Linguitt cradled in his arms and the Emamoose walked on the other side of Doodlebewshet, helping her across some of the rockier patches.

The point that divided this and the next cove was formed by a low hill covered in berry bushes and light green moss ending in a vertical cliff of rusty colored rock. The dejected little procession followed the narrow animal track that wound up the side of the hill.

Shanawdithit selected a place near the edge of the cliff where Linguitt would be overlooking the water. They scraped away the plants from the surface and laid Linguitt on the rock with her face to the sea. Doodlebewshet slipped a shell necklace from her neck and handed it to Shanawdithit to place next to Linguitt. Shanawdithit and the other two then covered her body with rocks until she was completely protected from any plundering wild animals.

Night had overtaken them and by the time they reached the Buggishaman's house what had seemed like a light summer rain had thoroughly soaked them to the bone. The trip had been difficult for Doodlebewshet. She had stumbled along supported between Shanawdithit and the Emamoose. They had taken many rests along the way and Shanawdithit had to do a lot of coaxing to keep her moving.

The Buggishaman had gone on ahead and had cleared out his shed by the time they arrived. He spread hay on the dirt floor and gave them extra blankets. It was dry and they were sheltered from the rain outside.

Later the Emamoose returned with some medicine for Doodlebewshet to drink to help with the coughing. After she left Shanawdithit lay there listening to the rain drumming on the roof until it lulled her to sleep.

That night, Shanawdithit was haunted by the dreams again. She was racing wildly through the woods. It was night but overhead a huge silver moon cast long dancing shadows on the ground around her. She could hear the panting and rustling in the bushes behind her and also out to her left. Her chest was scorching from within and her breath came in frantic gasps.

Suddenly, she broke free of the woods and sprinted out onto the silvery sand of the moonlit beach. In the distance, standing on the top of a hill, she could see a mound of stones. Her mother, Shanadee, stood next to it waving her on.

With renewed strength she ran across the wet sand toward her mother. Behind she could hear the sound of four feet loping across the sand. The beast was closer. The air was split with a bone-chilling howl. She felt her blood turn cold. The sand was clutching her feet slowing her down. She was close. She could see the encouragement in her mother's eyes and in her outstretched hand. She reached the path and began to scramble upwards on her knees when she felt the hot breath of the moisamadrook on the back of her neck. She rolled on her back and raised her hands protectively as it struck at her face. She screamed in terror.

The beast had gripped her by the shoulder and was shaking her.

In the distance she heard a voice speaking in a strange language, the Buggishaman language.

She opened her eyes and stared up into the Emamoose's face as she released her hand from Shanawdithit's shoulder. Still not fully awake, she looked around the shed at the dancing shadows cast by the light the Emamoose was carrying and shuddered as she remembered the dream. The air felt cool to her sweat covered skin and she drew the blanket a little tighter around her. Doodlebewshet lay sleeping on the other side of the shed. She had not been disturbed by the noise but Shanawdithit could see she was still breathing.

She smiled sheepishly at the Emamoose and lay back on the ground. The Emamoose patted her lightly on the shoulder and walked out the door, taking the light with her.

Shanawdithit lay there staring out the open door at the black sky overhead. It was filled with twinkling lights, some seemed to form designs. She could see a pot and a hathemay. The longer she stared the more things she saw. Her ancestors were out there somewhere. Sleep did not return and she watched the sky turn from black to gray. Then the rooster crowed, welcoming the new morning.

She pushed the blanket aside and walked down to the beach to the water's edge. Far out over the water, the sun peered over the edge as if checking to see if it was safe to come out. The water between them rippled in shades of orange and gold. It lifted her out of her sadness for a moment and she smiled at the beauty of the colors.

Behind her a door swung wide on its hinges and hit the outside wall. She turned and saw the Emamoose step out on the bridge of the house. She waved for her to join her and Shanawdithit left the beach and made her way up to the house. Before she reached the steps the Emamoose met her and, taking her by the arm, led her to the chicken coop. She reached inside the little box and brushed at one of the hens, knocking it from its nest. She picked up the two warm eggs and handed them to Shanawdithit then she shooed the next hen and retrieved two more eggs. The Emamoose continued to move around the box until she had emptied all the nests. Then she led Shanawdithit back to the house where she showed her how to crack the eggs and drop them into the hot pan. Quickly the kitchen was filled with mouth watering smells and the sizzle and pop of the frying eggs.

The Emamoose slid the cooked eggs onto two plates and set one before each of the two chairs at the small wooden table. She motioned Shanawdithit to sit in one of the chairs and she sat on the other one. She carved two slices from the loaf of bread, placed one on each of their plates, and began to eat.

Following her lead, Shanawdithit began to eat and didn't look up until her plate was empty, wiped out with the slice of bread, and each of her fingers had been licked clean. She had no idea she was so hungry. Suddenly she thought of Doodlebewshet and she felt guilty. As if reading her thoughts, the Emamoose walked back to the stove, picked up two more of the eggs, and held them out to Shanawdithit, pointing at the hot pan.

Shanawdithit took the eggs and broke them like she had seen the Emamoose do. The Emamoose laughed softly at her awkwardness and picked the pieces of broken shell from the pan. She helped Shanawdithit scrape the fried eggs onto a clean plate and watched from the door as she carried the plate of food down to the shed.

As she walked past the scratching hens Shanawdithit glanced at the wharf. The boat was no longer tied there. The Buggishaman must have left before the sun came up, she thought.

Stepping inside the shed, she found Doodlebewshet sitting on the floor with her back against the wall.

"Where have you been?" asked Doodlebewshet weakly.

"Up at the Buggishaman's house. The Emamoose showed me how to make these. They are for you."

"I don't think I can eat."

"You must. You have to get your strength up. I had some and they are good."

"I don't need it, Shanawdithit. It is time for me to make my journey to Gossett."

"Don't say that."

"I don't have the strength to stay any longer," she replied weakly as she struggled to suppress another cough. "I don't have anyone left. Linguitt is gone and I will not see Jaywritt and Aaduth again on this side. Maybe we will all find each other in the land of Gossett."

"Maybe, but you are here now and I need you to eat this."

She sat next to the old woman and lifted some of the egg to her mouth. Reluctantly, Doodlebewshet took the food and swallowed it. Shanawdithit helped her finish everything that was on the plate and then set it aside.

She wrapped her arms around her and cradled her head on her chest. "You have been a good mother to me, Doodlebewshet," she whispered. "You are all I have left and you must not leave me alone."

She began to hum softly until she felt Doodlebewshet had fallen asleep again. Gently, she laid her back on the blankets and left her there. Stepping outside the shed, she saw the Emamoose was in the vegetable garden. She went and joined her.

They spent the morning working together. The Emamoose showed Shanawdithit which ones were vegetable plants and which ones were weeds to be plucked out of the ground. Shanawdithit realized she was enjoying being around this Emamoose. Her stern exterior was not a reflection of the person who was inside.

They worked side by side until the sun reached the top of its journey, then the Emamoose stood to her feet and motioned to Shanawdithit to follow her back to the house. Inside she pulled out a chair for Shanawdithit to sit at the table and then set out baked buns and poured a hot dark liquid into mugs. She pushed one in front of Shanawdithit and watched as her guest tentatively sipped the steaming liquid. She smiled as Shanawdithit grimaced at the strong taste and reached out and dropped a spoon full of sugar into the mug. She stirred vigorously and pushed it back in front of Shanawdithit again.

This time Shanawdithit liked the taste better. She smiled as she felt the hot liquid trickling down her throat. She wondered how it could make her feel so contented.

"Tea," said the woman, pointing at the mug.

"Tea," repeated Shanawdithit.

After they finished eating, Shanawdithit returned to the shed to check on Doodlebewshet. The Emamoose followed close behind her, carrying more food.

As soon as she stepped through the door, she sensed something was wrong. Doodlebewshet was slumped against the wall. Shanawdithit ran to her, dropped to her knees, and gripped her by the shoulders. Shaking her, she cried "Doodlebewshet," as she stared into her face.

Doodlebewshet did not respond no matter how much she shook her.

She felt the Emamoose's hands on her shoulders gently pulling her away.

Doodlebewshet was gone. She had known all along. She tried to tell me, thought Shanawdithit.

She sat on the hay covered floor and sobbed quietly. The Emamoose sat beside her with her strong arm wrapped around her shoulder.

Sometime later the Buggishaman found them there.

Taking in the scene before him, he picked up the shovel that was sitting against the wall and walked out the door again.

Together they carried Doodlebewshet to the grave he had dug at the edge of the field and placed her in it. Shanawdithit covered her with the blanket. She placed the drawing she had made of their family in Doodlebewshet's hand.

The evening shadows accompanied them as she walked back to the house with the Emamoose. Before entering, she stopped and watched the Buggishaman shovel the last dirt on the grave and then hammer a small wooden marker in place.

She was alone.

A little more than a week later, John Peyton's schooner sailed into the cove and anchored off shore. A dory was lowered over the side and Peyton and another climbed in and rowed to the wharf. Peyton accompanied the Buggishaman up to the house where Shanawdithit and the Emamoose were working in the kitchen.

As they stepped through the door Shanawdithit looked up from the dough she was kneading. Her eyes met Peyton's and they recognized each other immediately. He smiled at her in surprise.

Turning to the Buggishaman, Peyton engaged in a long conversation with him that was obviously about her. She watched as the Buggishaman pointed out the window toward the place where Doodlebewshet was buried.

They seemed to come to an agreement that she would go with Peyton because the Emamoose began to gather Shanawdithit's things together. She placed them on a sheet, tied the corners together, and handed it to Shanawdithit. She wrapped her arms around Shanawdithit, held her close for a moment, and then stepped back. Peyton took her by the arm and led her out the door and down to the wharf.

Chapter 17
1827

Four years had passed since that terrible day in April when Aaduth found his friend Basadict. They had been busy years. Days were filled with work and evenings were filled with learning and laughter. Aaduth had grown accustomed to his new life with Andrew and Sarah. He was happy in his new home. Thanks to Sarah's untiring efforts he had learned many of the Buggishaman words and was growing more skilled with the language every day. He wanted to learn and worked very hard at it.

Sarah took every opportunity to share her love of books with Aaduth. Her library was small with a few Jane Austen books and one by Mary Shelly that seemed a little out of place to him, but the more he listened to it the more he learned to like it. She read it aloud to him often in the dim light of the flickering candles. In some strange way he felt a connection to

Frankenstein's monster. He had been the only one of his race just like Aaduth, who believed he was now the only Beothuk left alive. It was a lonely thought.

Long, stormy, winter days were passed discussing the stories while Andrew napped on the other side of the room. Sometimes he would lay there and just listen to their happy chatter against the background of the whirling wind outside. Life had become much more meaningful for him and Sarah since John had become a part of their family.

Sarah had introduced Aaduth to the pencil and paper this past winter. She was showing him how to form letters. He had watched Shanawdithit draw pictures on birch bark before but he had never seen anyone make marks on paper to represent the words they were speaking. It was fascinating to him. He was determined to master it one day.

"John," Sarah would always say, "you need to learn to do this so one day you can tell the stories of your people. They must never be forgotten. You are the only one left that can pass them on to your children."

One day when they were sitting at the little table with books and paper spread around, Sarah got up to retrieve her Bible from the stand next to the bed. She opened it to the *Family Record* section and showed him the page where she had added his name next to hers and Andrew's. It made him happy. He had a family again.

Aaduth had helped Andrew build on to the little cabin and now he had his own small room. It was only big enough for him to sleep in but he liked his time alone there. It had no window and the door was a blanket that slid on a wooden pole. He hung his hathemay on the wall over his bed along with Basadict's bag. Then in the corner of the room he placed his father's broken aaduth. Andrew had helped him cure the bearskin and he used it for a blanket. These were all he had to remind him of his past life.

The coastline was still sparsely populated and they did not often see other settlers. Once in a while there would be a chance meeting while out in the boat but nothing more than that. The only other people they saw were the traders that came by once a year during the summer. That was usually William Cull and his men. He lived out on a place called Barr'd Island, just off from Fogo. He operated a schooner and on his trips up to St. John's he picked up supplies for Andrew and some of the other settlers along the coast. They anchored the schooner farther out in the cove and came ashore in a smaller boat bringing flour, salt, and other essentials that they traded for Andrew's fish.

Aaduth always stayed hidden during those visits. Andrew and Sarah felt it was safer it not be known that he lived with them. There were still those that would kill Beothuks and there was a reward out of St. John's for anyone bringing in a live one. Sarah had heard that from Cull's own lips. He'd already captured a Beothuk woman a few years ago and taken her to St. John's. They had paid him good money, he'd said. Worth the trip, he figured. He didn't really hold to the St. John's idea of trying to establish relations with the Red Indians. She'd heard him say that sitting at this very kitchen table. And then there was the story he told of taking the three Beothuk women the same year John had been found by Andrew. He had left them with John Peyton on Exploits Island, he said. He found out shortly after that two of them died of consumption. Sarah had always wondered about those women, especially about what had become of the third one, but she chose not to tell John. Sometimes she felt guilty about it but she felt she was protecting him.

"I'll give him a cup a tea but I'll never allow John around him," she had said to Andrew after Cull had left. "I'm not taking any chances."

Over the years, Sarah had made him new clothes and convinced him to cut his hair shorter like Andrew's. The red ochre had disappeared and, although his skin was darker, he could probably pass for a white man but Sarah was too nervous to let him try.

"Maybe next year," she'd always say.

Aaduth was awaken by the soft sounds of Andrew quietly moving around in the other room. It was the signal for him to get up. Pushing back the bearskin covering, he quickly pulled on his shirt and trousers. For the past year he had been dressing the same as Andrew, in Buggishaman clothes. He had grown taller and bigger in four years and his clothes no longer fit. Sarah had made him new things to wear. He glanced at his old tunic hanging on the wall where Sarah had left it. Although she had washed it, probably more than once, there was still a faint red tint where it had been stained with the odemet (red ochre). It was a reminder of who he really was and he was glad she had kept it.

It was cold this morning and he didn't waste any time getting to the main room next to the warm stove.

"Morning, Son," Andrew whispered to him cheerfully.

"Morning," mumbled Aaduth as he struggled into the long rubber boots that were warming next to the stove. He had never quite gotten used to wearing them, having just worn moccasins or gone bare foot for most of his life. But they kept his feet dry and were a lot more comfortable when in the boat with the cold water sloshing around in the bottom.

"Be careful," he heard Sarah mumble sleepily from the bed in the corner as they walked out the door.

Like Aaduth, the day was only just waking up, but the faint morning light was enough to see it was promising to be another gray foggy day. He didn't like being on the water in the fog. Even though they had done it many times before, he hated how it disoriented him once the shore disappeared into the thick mist. Knowing Andrew could always find the way home was comforting but he still didn't like it. He could never rest until the sun had burnt it off or Andrew brought them safely back to the wharf.

"Looks like another foggy old day," observed Andrew as they pulled away from the wharf, their paddles dipping in unison. Andrew had added a second set of oar locks toward the back of the boat for Aaduth so they could both row, now that there was two of them.

The fog quickly closed in and the wharf was swallowed up behind them. The all too familiar feeling of dread settled down on Aaduth like a thick cloud, smothering him, and he tried to push it out of his mind and think of something else.

The only sounds were the water dripping from their paddles each time they swung out over the water and the cheerful refrain of Andrew's whistling.

They rowed out of the cove past the tall headland that marked its end. Aaduth couldn't see it but he knew it was there by the sound of the waves lapping against the sheer cliff walls. They were rowing straight across the bay to one of the large islands that separated it from the open ocean. Andrew had set his nets near a long sandy point that jutted out from a smaller island. They often went ashore on that beach and ate their lunch before returning home with the catch.

About an hour later Andrew brought them out of the fog just off the sandy point, within sight of the floating bobbers that marked the first of the three nets.

Andrew stored his paddles and waited for Aaduth to bring the boat alongside the lead float on the net. He hooked it into the boat and draped the line across the midsection. This would allow them to pull the net across the boat, emptying it of fish as they went. Like most days, the net was heavy in the water, filled with fish and it took their combined strength to pull it into the boat.

By the time they had emptied the third net the boat was riding low in the water. Slippery wriggling fish completely filled the centre box and spilled out onto the floor of the rest of the boat.

The wind had picked up some and was beginning to create whitecaps on the larger waves. Andrew looked up at the dark threatening sky and then at the disappearing fog bank off to the rear of the boat.

"I fear we are in for a blow, John my son," he said. "We had better get underway."

Aaduth helped him lift the small sail into place and they set out for home.

Nervously, Aaduth looked at the hazy blue shoreline in the distance. It was a long way to go. The wind was blowing off the land, pushing them farther off course. Using the sail, Andrew was steering them away from land. He never understood how sailing worked and why sometimes you had to steer away from where you wanted to go to get there. Andrew had tried to explain it to him but he just didn't get it. It made no sense, especially in this wind. The quicker they could get ashore the better.

They switched places and Andrew was now at the back of the boat with one hand on the tiller and the other firmly grasping the sail line. Aaduth sat at the front facing forward with a firm grip on the seat where Andrew had been rowing, anxiously watching the waves.

In the time it had taken them to switch and get underway the wind had come racing in from behind and filled the sail, straining the material on its bindings. The heavily laden boat was riding so low in the water that the waves were constantly washing over the side and the salty spray had soaked them both in minutes. Aaduth dropped to his knees, grabbed the wooden bucket, and began bailing as fast as he could. The wind was roaring now, angrily assaulting the little sail standing in its way. Aaduth glanced up at Andrew and the look of concern on his face frightened him. He had never seen Andrew look that way before. They should have gone ashore on the island and waited it out but now they were so far offshore there was no chance of getting back there. He went back to bailing in earnest.

Out of the corner of his eye he saw a larger wave bearing down on them. The bailing bucket slipped from his hand. He grabbed the side of the boat with both hands and ducked down. Andrew had also seen it coming and managed to steer partially into it, but the jarring impact when it did hit the boat yanked the sail line from his hand. Half standing he grabbed for it, slipped on the fish as the boat rolled over the wave, and went over the side, cracking his head on the gunwale as he fell.

"Andrew," yelled Aaduth.

Ducking under the wildly swinging boom, Aaduth crawled to the back of the boat and peered into the black water. Andrew was nowhere to be seen. Even though the sail was no longer full the momentum was carrying the boat away from the spot where Andrew had gone overboard. Three of the paddles had been knocked out of the boat by the waves and were floating away astern. The sail had pulled through its lashings and was flapping wildly in the wind. Water was washing in over the side of the floundering boat. He was in danger of sinking. He had to get that sail down as quickly as he could.

Desperately, he scanned the water again for Andrew. He knew Andrew, like him, had never learned to swim. He could see no sign of him but he did spot one of the paddles, now far astern.

The boat was wallowing in the deep swell and the sail boom swung wildly back and forth across the boat, threatening to knock Aaduth into the water. There was so much water in the boat now some of the fish were floating. Fighting against the violent rolling, Aaduth crawled through the slippery fish to the sail mast. On his second attempt he managed to grab the whipping sail line and haul the canvas tight against the mast, winding it around and tying it off. The boom line was still attached so he pulled the boom vertical and secured it. It would make the boat more stable if he could lift the mast out of its footing but he knew he wasn't going to be able to do that by himself; certainly not in these seas. Anyway, the boat was no longer behaving so unpredictably as before. He began to bail again. This time both fish and water were thrown overboard.

The waves were no longer washing in over the side so he finally started making headway with bailing. When he'd gotten it down to a reasonable level, he threw the bucket down and knelt there holding the gunwale on each side of the boat, waiting for his breathing to slow and his heart to stop racing. He gazed around him at the large waves that were striking the boat, threatening to roll it on its side. He needed to head the boat into those waves like Andrew had taught him. Crawling back over the remaining fish in the open midsection, he reached the stern where the tiller was swinging freely with the action of the waves. Grabbing it with both hands, he attempted to turn the boat into the waves but it wouldn't respond. He tried to think how Andrew had done this. He remembered Andrew telling him something about the boat moving. Yes, that was it. It had to be moving forward or backward for the tiller to work. He reached for the one remaining paddle and pushed it through the sculling hole until there was only a little more than the length of his arm inside the boat. With the paddle extended so far out in the water he was finally able to stabilize it and eventually bring it around into the wind.

With most of the fish still in the boat it still rode low in the water but it was no longer rolling with the waves. It was stable enough for him to risk standing. He placed his feet wide apart and pushed to a standing position while keeping a good grip on his one remaining paddle.

"Andrew," he shouted as he scanned the water again looking for some sign of him.

"Andrew!"

Apart from the howling wind there was no sound, no answer from Andrew.

He had no idea how far the boat had drifted since Andrew had gone over the side but he knew it was nowhere near the spot now.

Slowly and carefully he studied the angry sea in every direction. There was nothing afloat; neither Andrew nor the paddles that he had lost. He slumped back down in the seat in despair. He knew then that the sea was not going to give Andrew back.

The memory of Sarah telling them to be careful earlier this morning flashed in his mind. She would be devastated. Andrew was her life. How would she continue without him? He knew it would fall on his shoulders to step in and try to take his place, at least as much as he could. But he would have to get ashore first, and he was a long way from that right now. The waves were pushing him farther away from the shore by the minute. He realized he would have to try rowing with the one paddle.

He tied the tiller in the straight position, pulled the paddle all the way into the boat, and shoved it toward the front seat. Then he crawled forward and set it in the left oarlock. He began to pull on the paddle, first on the left and then on the right, changing sides after every couple of pulls.

It was back-breaking work, and the sea fought hard to claim him for itself, but he stubbornly kept at it. At first he didn't seem to be making any progress but after a while he worked up a rhythm and the boat actually felt like it was beginning to inch forward. He glanced over his shoulder at the land way off in the distance. It was so far he was not sure he would have been able to see someone if they were standing on the beach.

A cold fear washed over him, forming little bumps up and down his arms. Suddenly he was not sure he could do this. Save for the lone sea bird circling high overhead, he was all alone out here. There was no one to help him and it was too much for him.

A picture of Sarah standing on the deck, anxiously looking out to sea began to form in his mind and he turned and faced the back of the boat again. He determined he wouldn't look at the shoreline again until he was sure he was closer. He returned to fighting the sea, a little more angrily this time.

What must have been an hour later his hands were bleeding and the pain in his back was almost unbearable. It seemed that he hadn't made much progress but the wind was easing off to make way for the approaching evening.

He rested the paddle across the boat and wound a strip of old cloth around each of his blistered hands. His grip wouldn't be as firm on the paddle but without the protection of the cloth he wouldn't be able to row much longer. Before continuing he took a quick look over his shoulder again and was surprised at the progress he had made. Details of the coves and beaches were clear now. He found the point of land that was closest, set the bloodstained handle of the paddle in the oarlock, and with a renewed hope began to row the boat towards it. With luck I might be able to reach the shoreline before dark, he thought.

He still occasionally called Andrew's name as he had been doing since he had seen him go overboard. He knew he would not get an answer after all this time but he tried anyway. Doing battle with the sea all afternoon had left him little time to think of Andrew but now that the worst of it seemed to be over, thoughts of him crowded into his weary mind. As he continued to pull the boat toward land the memories flooded in. Tears fell from his eyes and began to trickle down over his salt stained face as he remembered.

Andrew's gentle and kind nature had been apparent to him from the first time he looked in his eyes along the length of his drawn arrow, the day Andrew rescued him from the great white washawet. He had nurtured him in his quiet and calm way, encouraging and teaching him not only how to fish and handle a boat but, by his example, the importance of family. Andrew had become his second father. He would miss him terribly but he would be proud to carry on his name.

Then there was Sarah. He knew she wouldn't take this news well. She would have expected them back by now. She would be at the window or outside on the deck worriedly wringing her hands in her apron, gazing out to sea, willing the boat to appear around the point. She would have probably gone to her Bible more than once by now.

Doggedly, he kept up the rhythm, first one side then the next, pushing through the pain that racked his sore aching muscles and burned his blistered hands. He focused on each stroke of the paddle and nothing else.

The day crawled by. The pain grew worse. His motions were now mechanical, without thought. He willed himself to keep going. He managed to drink from the water bottle without losing his rhythm. He knew if he stopped he probably wouldn't start again.

He remembered the stories he had heard at the nightly campfire. It was believed that if a Beothuk did evil a great monster would come from the sea and swallow him up. Was that what happened to Andrew? he wondered. He nervously looked at the dark water around the boat.

Why would it come for Andrew? He was not an evil man. Perhaps it mistook him. Maybe it would return for him. He tried to remember the prayers he had heard to ward off the monster. He repeated what he could remember. He even prayed to Sarah's god the way he had heard Sarah do time and time again. He was ready to take help from anyone now.

As the evening gradually settled around him the wind all but disappeared. He could hear the smaller waves lapping against the sheer face of the cliff that defined the point, which had been invisible in the early morning fog. He was almost home. He was going to make it. He was afraid to believe it.

Before long he was within a boat length of the cliff face. He edged the boat along the face, keeping his distance from the rocks until he reached a place where a rocky beach marked the end of a gently sloping meadow. It was the best thing he had seen in days. When the boat touched the rocky bottom he stumbled over the side into the shallow water, pulled the keel onto the beach, and tied the painter to an old tree stump. He crawled on his knees for a couple of feet until he reached the grass and then he collapsed in exhaustion.

He lay there on his face for a long time without moving. Tears of relief filled his eyes as he sniffed the welcoming earth beneath his nose. He licked his lips to remove the coating of salt the sea had left him. The ordeal had taken everything from him but he had survived.

Finally, he rolled over on his back in the short grass and looked up at the canopy of twinkling lights. He wondered if Andrew was one of them. He knew his ancestors were up there. He hoped they would welcome Andrew. Scanning the sky, he picked a particularly bright light and decided that would be the one. From now on he would always look at that light and remember Andrew.

Sitting up, he looked across the harbour and saw another twinkling light. It was coming from the window of Andrew and Sarah's house. No sight had ever been so welcome to him. He slowly became aware of the wide grin that had crept across his tired face. Then he remembered the news he had to bring to Sarah.

In the low bushes to his left the muted sounds of night song birds reminded him that he was on land again and that he had won the battle the sea had raged against him all day long.

Chapter 18
1827

Life had been so different since John had returned from his second trip up the coast. Life had been good when it was just her and Andrew but there had always been something missing. John had filled that little piece of emptiness for her. He had completed the family she had always dreamed of having.

There had been times she had felt the loneliness of being separated from her birthplace and her family by so great a distance, especially during the long winter months when there was little else to do than watch time go by. Having John here took much of that away. Times were busy. There was always something to do. Busy times were happy times.

This was a lonely, remote land surrounded by an untamed and often angry sea. Sometimes months went by without having contact with another living soul. It was a harsh land but she had learned to love its ruggedness and unspoiled beauty. Their little horse shoe cove was defined on one end by a point of sheer tan-colored rock cliff rising about fifty feet into the air and on the other side by a low point that projected far out into the water. The sheltered cove had low sloping tree-covered hills that gently rolled down to the rocky beach. Every fall the hills were transformed into a blaze of color as the leaves prepared to abandon the trees that brought them to life and had nurtured them through the summer. She loved the colors, from the deep reds to the softer oranges and yellows. She had collected many of them and pressed them between the pages of her Bible. Even though nature's colorful painting heralded the fast approaching winter, she loved the fall season the best.

There was a quiet peacefulness about this life they had carved out of the barren coast. Lying in bed at night listening to the waves rattling over the beach rock was a comforting sound, a familiar sound that made this place feel like home.

It had not taken long to realize the island did not give up its bounty easily. The thin rocky soil of the cold windswept coast was not ideal for planting but they learned, with persistence and hard work, it could be coaxed to give back. Over the years they had cleared enough land behind the house to grow the vegetables they needed to get them through the winters. Sarah spent many long hours there while Andrew tended his nets and fishing lines.

Now that John was here they were able to do more with their land. He was a big help to Andrew and a willing helper. Together they had cleared more land and set it with potatoes, carrots, and a row of cabbage. That would make for a better winter this year.

She loved to watch them working together like father and son. Well, he was their son as far as she was concerned and he sure seemed to have bonded with Andrew. He was good for Andrew and Andrew was good for him.

She had always wondered about the Beothuks but she had never seen one until now. She had heard the stories about how they couldn't be trusted and would steal everything you had. Others said they were dangerous and you should shoot first and ask questions later. It was said there were hunters who trapped in the interior who bragged about how many Beothuk, or Red Indians as some called them, they had killed. She had never thought that was right. The Indians were people just like the rest of us. They deserved to be left alone. Old William Cull had sat in this very kitchen and said there were none of them left, that they had all been killed off. And even if that's not true he had said that the few that might be around have gone back into the country where they will starve to death before too long. Sarah felt sad about that. She didn't like that man.

Now that she had John she felt nothing but anger and disgust at that kind of thinking and she would be doing whatever was necessary to protect him from those people. That's why she had convinced him to cut his hair and stop rubbing the red ochre on his skin. She had made him clothes like Andrew's as well, but that was necessary anyway since he had grown out of his own. No one but she and Andrew would know he was Beothuk. The rest of the world would believe he was their rightful son. It would be a secret they would take to their graves.

Much of her time had been spent teaching John the language. That had proved to be some of the best times of her life. John was eager to learn and she found teaching was something that came easy to her. Those were fun times in the evenings when the day's work was done. It was a time they both looked forward to. She loved to watch the look of pride on his face when he mastered a new word or strung them together to make a sentence. Most times he would wake Andrew from his nap to try out what he had learned. Their laughter was musical to her. There is a lot of laughter here these days, she thought, smiling to herself.

She glanced out the window again. The evening was closing in and darkness was drifting down from the hills. They should have been back by now. They were never this late. Perhaps the wind had slowed them down. She stepped out on the deck and stared out across the cove again, just as she had done a dozen times in the last hour.

The wind had been blowing so hard earlier this afternoon that it had forced her to take the clothes in from the line for fear some of it would end up across the harbour. It had blown itself out a while ago and it was now a quiet evening. She hadn't worried about the wind being a problem for the boys at the time. They had been out in worse. But now she wondered, what if something had happened to them.

There was nothing to be seen out there. Wringing her hands in her apron, she turned and went back into the kitchen. She tried to get back to cooking the meal, knowing they would be starving when they came ashore, but she couldn't put her mind to it. Her hands were sweating and her heart was beating much faster than it should. She couldn't keep her eyes away from the window. Something was wrong, she just knew. In frustration she went out on the deck again, leaving the door open behind her. It was much darker now. They would be able to see the light, she thought, even though she knew Andrew had a great sense of direction and would have no problem finding his way home.

Where were they? She looked back through the open door and her eyes fell on the open Bible laying on the kitchen table.

"Protect them Lord," she said aloud. "Bring them home safe."

Perhaps they had gone ashore and waited for the wind to blow over. She really shouldn't be worried about them yet. They were probably out there in the bay now and she couldn't see them in the dark. She paced the length of the deck, stopping at each end to rest her hands on the rail while she peered into the dark. The only sound was the quiet lapping of the water down on the beach and soft chirping of night birds out behind the house.

Aaduth lay on the damp grass, leaning back on his elbows. He looked across the cove at the tiny square of welcoming light that marked Andrew and Sarah's house. He could get the boat across to the wharf; it wasn't that far. But now that he was out of the boat he just didn't want to get back in it. Anyway, his hands were in too much of a mess to do any more rowing tonight.

The fish would have to keep until morning and if they didn't so be it. He still had to face Sarah and give her the news about Andrew. The fish really weren't all that important right now.

It seemed there wasn't a part of his body that didn't hurt. Trying his best to push past the pain, he gingerly pushed his cramped body to its feet and started walking. He had to pick his way around the larger rocks that were strewn around the beach, seeming to be carefully placed there by some giant hand, yet in a completely random pattern. Overhead, the partial moon provided just enough light for him to avoid the small pools left behind by the receding tide. The tangy smell of decaying seaweed filled the air around him. All was quiet except for the squelch of his boots as he trudged along through patches of wet mud that defined large stretches of the shoreline.

Now that he wasn't fighting the sea he had time to think of Andrew. It wasn't that he hadn't seen death before, in fact he had seen a lot of it in his young life. His people had been losing the battle for survival for years. But he had grown close to this Buggishaman. He was going to miss him more than he cared to think.

It would be up to him to take care of Sarah now. That's what Andrew would expect of him.

As he got closer to the cabin, he could hear Sarah rattling things in the kitchen. The door was wide open and the smell of cooked supper washed over him as he walked up the steps to the deck.

Sarah must have heard him because she turned with a startled look and the dish she was holding fell to the floor with a crash. Her hand flew to her mouth as she rushed across the room and out onto the deck. She stopped before she reached Aaduth and looked over his shoulder toward the wharf. Her eyes returned to his. She gasped in anguish as she saw the answer to her unasked question. She stumbled and slumped back into the deck chair in despair.

"No, John. No," she wailed through the hands that covered her face. "Please John, no," she moaned as she rocked back and forth in the chair.

Aaduth moved to her side and gently wrapped his arm around her trembling shoulder.

"Oh Andrew, not now when everything is going so good," she sobbed. "You can't leave us now."

Tears streamed down her face as she looked up at Aaduth then, as if noticing for the first time, she grabbed one of his wrapped hands.

"What happened to you?" she asked, staring at the blood soaked cloth covering both of his hands. Hastily wiping her eyes with her apron, she jumped to her feet and dragged him by the arm through the doorway into the kitchen.

She sat him in a chair and carefully unwrapped the bloody cloth, revealing his blistered and bleeding hands.

"You rowed ashore by yourself, didn't you?"

"I only had one paddle," he replied.

Sarah stared at him in amazement as she lifted the pot from the stove. She poured warm water into a shallow wash basin and added a sprinkle of salt.

"You poor boy," she muttered. "Here, soak your hands in this for a while. We need to make sure they are clean.

Gingerly, he slipped his left hand into the water quickly followed by his right, all the while grimacing at the sting. A soft moan slipped through his lips.

Sarah watched him with concern. "Better a little pain now, John, than have them get infected later."

"I suppose you haven't eaten yet today, have you?"

Aaduth shook his head, no.

Sarah spooned food from the boiling pot onto a plate and placed it in front of him. He glanced at the other two plates on the table and a fresh tear escaped from the corner of his eye and trickled down his cheek.

Sarah reached out and blotted it with her thumb. Tenderly, she placed her hand on his head and kissed him on the cheek.

Before letting him eat she rubbed salve on his hands and wrapped them with fresh, clean bandages. "Tomorrow we'll take the bandages off and let the air get at those hands," she said. "They'll be healed up in no time."

As he began to awkwardly eat with his bandaged hands, Sarah left him and went to sit outside on the deck.

Aaduth could hear her sobbing softly.

He swallowed hard past the lump in his throat, bent his head, and concentrated on the stew. He knew this was where he would be staying. He would be John Foss from now on.

Chapter 19
1828

Five long years had slowly dragged by since he had taken his family and abandoned his mother and father at the old camp by the Great River. He had returned there only once. Once had been enough. Something had changed in him after that visit.

He had waited until the following spring, not wanting to risk exposing himself to the disease that had claimed his father, mother, and sister. He wanted to be sure he didn't bring it back to his family. They were all he had left. In fact, they were the only Beothuks he knew were still alive.

On arriving at the old campsite it was clear none of the tribe members that had left the camp before him had ever returned. The camp did not appear to have been lived in since his parents and sister had died. The two mamateeks were ragged, peppered with holes and in need of much repair. The birch rind lining the outside had cracked and torn in places and was flapping wildly in the wind, as if frantically waving him away from the door and what he would find inside.

Despite his overwhelming feeling of dread, he had pushed aside the remnants of the caribou skin door to his parent's mamateek and stepped across the threshold.

The three of them were there; at least what remained of them. Animals had visited them since he had been away. They had no protection. There was no one left to prepare them for their journey and they had been left where they died.

There had been no sign of little Ebanthou. He had searched the other mamateek and all around the camp but found no trace. He wondered what had happened to her. Perhaps the animals had taken her away. He hoped she had not been the last to go. He remembered standing in the middle of the campsite and shuddering at the thoughts that crowded his mind. Suppose she had been left on her own, all alone and afraid. How could she have survived on her own? She couldn't. He would find that he would never escape the thing that took root in his mind that day. It was a living thing that nurtured itself on the guilt he felt over abandoning them to die.

He had done his best to arrange what was left of his mother, father, and sister, to help their spirits find their way into the land of Gossett. Once he finished he ignited the mamateek and watched it burn around them. The embers were still glowing throughout the ash heap when he had walked out of the clearing, never to return to that place again. It was not a good place. There was nothing left for him there, only bitter reminders of his failure as a son.

Langnon had built a new camp for his small family. This time it was much closer to the coast. There were only four of them so they didn't need much, just the one mamateek. It was on the outskirts of a small settlement and they had not had any conflict with the Buggishaman who lived there. Still, they took care to avoid contact as much as possible. He would never fully trust the Buggishaman. It was because of the Buggishaman he could count the tribe on one hand. They had come to this land with their guns and diseases and killed them all. Why would he trust them? They just took what they wanted as if it were free for the taking. There was no thought that the Beothuk were here first; just a nuisance to be pushed aside.

There were days he thought he should just push back, maybe make them pay for all the family members he had lost to them. He knew it was a fight he could never win but perhaps that didn't matter anymore.

His thoughts drifted back to earlier this year, the time when the spring thaw sent great chunks of ice rocketing down the Great River. His sister-in-law, Hanawadet, had joined a band of Micmac Indians who were trekking across the island to the south coast. She had been smitten by one of the young men in their camp and agreed to go with him. Parting with her sister and nephew, Jiggameel, had been tearful, both sides struggling with the knowledge that they would not likely see each other again. As for him, he really didn't feel the loss. She had undoubtedly supported her sister in abandoning his parents at the old camp. Maybe Godabonyee would be less pushy with her biggest supporter gone.

There was only three of them now; him, his wife, and their son. A tiny remnant of a once great nation. In his short lifetime he had watched the tribe dwindle to where it was today, practically non-existent.

He wished he had lived back when there were so many Beothuk that they had covered most of the island. That was before the Buggishaman. Things seemed to have been much easier then. Now all he had left were the stories and no one to tell them to.

He often tried to relate the stories to Jiggameel but he wasn't sure how much the boy understood with his hearing problem. Probably not very much at all.

Langnon often wondered what it was like not to hear any sound at all. But then Jiggameel had never heard the birds singing in the trees or the waves crashing on the sea shore or even his mother's voice, so he guessed he couldn't miss what he'd never had. He seemed to be happy and his problem didn't keep him from doing what most boys his age did.

Whether it was compensation for his loss or simply not understanding the danger, Jiggameel had shown himself to be fearless when it came to climbing. He had seen his son climb a sheer cliff face without hesitation just because it was there. Langnon shuddered at the memory. He had no stomach for heights and he remembered the cold sweat of fear trickling down his back as he watched his son from the beach below until he had disappeared over the top of the cliff. Moments later he had reappeared, standing nonchalantly at the very edge, waving down to him. Langnon had no desire to see that again.

Today he and Jiggameel were on the way to the coast to gather shellfish. It was early when they left the camp. Godabonyee was still sleeping and they had been careful not to disturb her as they left the mamateek in the darkness before dawn.

The sun had not yet appeared in the sky and the morning dew sprinkled their feet as they brushed the grass in their passing. They had to carefully pick their way through the trail as it passed through the woods, where the light of the coming day had not yet penetrated.

They walked the familiar trail in silence as if they both lived in Jiggameel's soundless world.

Langnon watched his son as he followed him along the worn animal path. He noticed how he reached out and touched the different trees and plants along the way as if registering them in his memory. The long braid hanging down his back swayed back and forth as his head turned from side to side in an effort not to miss anything around him. He had taken to wearing a blue jay feather at the crown of his head where the braid began. It had started when Langnon had told him about Shanawdithit's father, Kirradittii, and how he had been known by the blue jay feather he always wore in his hair. He must be understanding some of the stories I try to tell him, thought Langnon.

A half smile creased his face when his eyes landed on the small bag of stones hanging on his son's side. He never went anywhere without those. They had gathered them from the beach on a previous trip, carefully selecting the roundest stones they could find. He remembered that day and how many stones were thrown away until Jiggameel was satisfied with the handful that now filled the little bag.

It was a game they played often. Sometimes his mother joined in as well, but it was not often either of them could beat Jiggameel anymore.

A small hole was scooped out of the ground, about the size of Langnon's fist. A line was drawn in the dirt exactly five strides away from the hole. Jiggameel always measured this very carefully just before he divided up the stones, giving half to his father and keeping half for himself.

Standing with a toe on the line, they would each take turns tossing the stones in an attempt to land them in the hole. The one with the closest stone got first chance to roll each of his stones into the hole by nudging them with his finger until he missed one. Then the other player took a turn. The winner was the one who landed all his stones in the hole first.

He loved the joy on Jiggameel's face and the sounds he made when he won. Sometimes he danced around in his excitement.

Just ahead, Jiggameel had turned and looked at his father. He swept his hand around his mouth and lifted his shoulders, asking, "Why are you smiling"?

Langnon touched his hand to his hip, indicating the bag of stones.

Jiggameel smiled, held a closed fist in the air, uttered his unique sound of triumph, and continued following the path.

Near the coast they skirted around a large field that had been claimed by the Buggishaman. Long rows of dirt with shallow trenches on each side ran the length of the field. Short green stalks were sticking through the ground along the rows. Langnon recognized them as potato plants. In a few weeks he would come back and dig up some of those potatoes. The Buggishaman could spare them.

They stayed close to the treeline that marked the edge of the field and then cut through the woods to the next cove. Out on the bay the sun was floating at the very edge of the water. Tiny fingers of mist dotted the quiet water of the cove where the warmth of the sun had not yet touched its surface.

A small island sat in the middle of the cove. It was peppered with a handful of short, misshapen evergreen trees stubbornly growing from cracks in the rocks that jutted out of the water. When the tide was out a narrow sandbar connected the island with the mainland. But now, as they walked the sandbar, they pushed through water that was as high as Jiggameel's knees.

Langnon was leading this time. He had crossed this sandbar many times before. Two large bags were slung over his shoulder to carry back the seashells. He walked with his thumbs hooked through the straps, which Godabonyee had decorated with strips of colored cloth she had taken from the Buggishaman.

Once they reached the island Langnon continued to the back side to stay out of sight of anyone watching from the mainland. Although he didn't expect trouble from the Buggishaman around here, he always thought it best to be safe and stay out of sight.

On this side of the island the water was deeper and the sea bed was formed by large boulders. Clusters of seashells had attached themselves to these rocks and it was a simple matter of wading into the water and pulling them free. The water was at the level of Langnon's chest so he was the one to go in and gather the seashells. Jiggameel filled the bags with the clusters his father threw to him. In a few minutes the bags were full and Langnon pulled himself out of the water and sat on a flat rock waiting for the sun to dry his sodden clothes. Jiggameel went off to explore the tiny island. Langnon sat there with his back propped against a large boulder, watching the sails of a boat far out on the bay as it slowly crossed from left to right in front of him. He wondered who they were and where they were going. He had never been on a large boat like that. He thought he might like to try it sometime.

When Jiggameel returned he touched his father's shoulder to wake him. The warm sun had dried his clothes as he slept. Shaking his head to rid himself of the cobwebs, Langnon gathered up the bags and led the way back to the sandbar, which was no longer fully submerged.

Once they reached the end of the sandbar he turned and followed the beach instead of returning to the path they had travelled before. He knew of a place nearby where seabirds nested atop the cliffs and they had plenty of time to harvest a few eggs before returning to camp.

As they travelled along the beach the sand changed to rocks and the rocks to boulders and soon they were walking along the edge of cliffs that soared up from the swirling water washing against the rocky base far below, just as he imagined it had long before he was born. He wondered how many of his ancestors had walked this same trail.

Overhead, several birds screeched their annoyance at being disturbed from their nests, occasionally dive bombing the intruders in an attempt to drive them away. Langnon swung a stick at the ones that came too close while Jiggameel, unaffected by the clamor, went about gathering the eggs.

Some of the birds had built their nests in the brush that grew out of the edge of the cliff overhanging the water below. Even those were not safe from Jiggameel. He lay on his stomach, reaching over the edge into the nests as if the sheer drop wasn't even there. The wind sweeping up the cliff face dislodged the blue feather from his braid and swept it along the ground until it fluttered to rest near Langnon's feet.

An unusually bold seabird was making a second dive at Langnon's face when he noticed with relief that Jiggameel was finished gathering eggs, had pushed himself back from the edge, and was standing to his feet. Swinging the stick wildly, Langnon grazed the big bird, knocking it off course and directly into the face of a shocked Jiggameel as it struggled to stay airborne. The weight of the flapping bird pushed Jiggameel backward as he clutched at its flailing wings. Langnon watched in horror as his son, wrestling with the bird, disappeared over the edge.

"Jiggameel," he screamed as he dropped to his knees and crawled to the edge, pulling himself on his stomach the last few feet.

As Langnon looked out over the edge, he saw the bag of eggs that had snagged on a tree growing out of the cliff, about an arm length below the edge. His head swam and his stomach rolled as he looked down past the dangling bag to the jagged rocks far below. He watched as a large wave crashed over the rock where his son's broken body lay, pulling him into the sea. His heart was beating out of his chest and he struggled to find a breath, even his lungs were crippled with fear. Fighting the nausea creeping up his throat, he lay there watching the water for some sign of Jiggameel. The sea remained empty.

Langnon pushed himself backward until he was no longer looking over the edge and buried his face in the short grass. His only son was gone.

The wind whisked the blue feather along the ground until it came to rest against the side of his face. He grasped it with his fingers as the tears blurred his vision.

Sometime later he pushed to his feet, picked up the remaining bag, took one last look at the edge of the cliff and began the long walk home.

The sun beat down on him from a cloudless sky but it provided him no comfort; the bright rays just stung his watery eyes. His world had turned gray and empty. There was nothing good about it. He gave no thought to his steps, simply placing one foot in front of the other. Instinctively he returned the way he had come, fiercely clutching the blue feather in his hand.

He did not want to think. He had lost everything. Just like every Beothuk before him, everything had been taken from him.

The seashells were heavy on his shoulder and his thoughts were heavy on his mind. The voices started muttering in his head again.

Chapter 20
1831

Godabonyee was trudging along the trail that would lead her back to camp. She had passed the day gathering berries and the bag she had slung over her shoulder was filled with ripe, juicy blueberries. It had been a long day of backbreaking work and she was bone tired. She was looking forward to sleep.

A soft wind rustled the leaves of the trees on either side of the path. It was enough to cool her heated skin and she lifted her face to the refreshing breeze in appreciation.

Rounding a bend in the trail, she came face to face with an Emamoose holding an Emamooset (white girl) by the hand. The Emamooset was sobbing softly and when she saw the Beothuk woman standing in front of her she began to cry in earnest.

The Emamoose eyed Godabonyee suspiciously and protectively drew the Emamooset against her side as she moved back a step. It was then Godabonyee noticed the little one only had one shoe.

Her other foot was wrapped in a blood-stained bandage made from a strip of the Emamoose's dress. She was putting all her weight on her one good foot.

Pointing at the bloody foot Godabonyee asked, "What happened?"

The Emamoose seemed to understand and placed her wrists against each other and snapped her hands together.

"A Buggishaman's trap," muttered Godabonyee. Why are they walking deeper into the woods away from the coast? she wondered.

"Where are you going?" she asked the Emamoose.

The Emamoose stared at her blankly.

Godabonyee dropped the berries and pointed back the way they had come and then the way she had come. She folded her hands and placed them against her cheek, tilting her head in the sleep position.

The Emamoose shrugged her shoulders and turned her hands palms up.

They are lost, realized Godabonyee.

Again she pointed back the way they had come, picked up the berries and walked past them. After a few steps she stopped and waited. The Emamoose stared at her with indecision in her eyes. The Emamooset peeked at her from behind her mother's skirts.

Finally reaching a decision, she grasped her whimpering daughter by the hand and began to follow Godabonyee.

The little one began to wail again.

Godabonyee stopped and dropped down on one knee until they caught up to her. She dipped her hand into her bag, drew out some blueberries, and offered them to the Emamooset.

She stared at Godabonyee through tear-filled eyes, looked up at her mother, and then hesitantly reached out and took several of the blueberries and popped them into her mouth. A shy smile slowly spread across her tear-streaked face and she reached for the rest.

Godabonyee glanced up at the Emamoose. Her eyes were smiling as well.

Godabonyee pushed herself to her feet. She pointed at the Emamooset and then placed her hand on her belly. The Emamoose smiled knowingly and nodded.

Godabonyee turned and led them down the path toward the settlement. When they were near her camp she hung the bag of blueberries from a tree branch and led them onto a side path that circled around the clearing. She did not want Langnon to know she was with the Emamoose. He had warned her not to have any contact with Buggishaman. She knew if he found out he would be angry again. She did not want that.

He had not been the same since losing Jiggameel. It was as if something had died inside him that horrible day. The least little thing could set him off and it usually turned physical. Most arguments ended in her getting hit, and arguments were frequent. There was nothing good between them anymore.

She'd hoped the news of the little one growing inside her would have made things better but it hadn't. He had gone into one of those dark places he sometimes retreated to. This one lasted for days. His rage had scared her and she stayed away from the mamateek until she felt it was safe.

He had warned her if she didn't find a way to get rid of it then he would. She didn't think he would actually kill the child but then this wasn't the Langnon she had married. She just didn't know what he was capable of. It made her very nervous.

She knew he blamed her for abandoning his family back at the Great River camp. What choice did she have? They would all have gotten the Buggishaman coughing disease and died like his parents and sister had. She had not been willing to risk that for Jiggameel.

The sight of smoke rising above the trees in the distance brought Godabonyee's thoughts back to the present. It was a sign they were nearing the settlement. It was as far as Godabonyee wanted to go. She stopped at a fork in the path and pointed out the one the Emamoose should take to get home and then turned to go. The Emamoose grabbed her by the hand and thanked her in their strange language. It was easy to see the gratitude in her eyes. The Emamooset smiled and waved at her as she limped away, holding tightly to her mother's hand.

With a sigh, Godabonyee turned and headed back to camp.

During the summer, Godabonyee returned to that place and watched the two of them as they worked and played in the garden. She loved to listen to the little one's laughter as she ran and danced around. It stirred her maternal instincts and she often held her hand over her own child that was growing in her belly as she watched.

One day the Emamooset spotted her sitting there and ran toward her. Her mother shouted for her to stop and then, seeing Godabonyee at the edge of the woods, she dropped her garden hoe and followed her daughter.

The Emamooset ran up to Godabonyee, grasped her by the hand, and pulled her towards her mother.

Godabonyee let the little one lead her and they all met in the middle of the vegetable garden.

Throughout the summer she returned there many times. She learned the Emamoose and her family were called Manual.

She was always very careful to hide her trips to the settlement from Langnon. It wasn't difficult these days. He had very little interest in anything and spent much of his time sitting by the fire in the mamateek, or sleeping.

Other times he would be gone for days without her knowing where he was. Sometimes he would return with wild game but many times with nothing. She suspected that at those times he had returned to the coast where he lost Jiggameel but he never said. He rarely said anything.

Godabonyee looked across the mamateek at her husband. He had only seen thirty-four winters, yet he was an old man. His leathery weather-lined face was drawn and tight with the grief he had never been able to let go. His long hair, once oily black and carefully braided, barely hung to his shoulders in ragged strands. He had hacked it off when it had turned white just weeks after he had returned from the coast without their son. They no longer lived, they simply existed.

She remembered that day when he stumbled into the clearing clutching the blue jay feather in his closed fist. Tears had washed the odemet from his face in jagged streaks and he was bent and beaten. Without asking she knew their son was gone.

She had led him into the mamateek where he brokenly sobbed out the story. He had blamed himself for Jiggameel's death then and he still did today.

Shortly after, he built a second mamateek and moved everything of Jiggameel's into it. Much of his days were spent sitting on the ground in that mamateek with his son's things spread around him.

She knew this was not good for Langnon, and many times when he was away from the camp she had considered burning the mamateek to release him. She had never done it. She missed her son too but mostly she feared what he would do to her and their unborn child.

He still hunted and provided food for them but there was no joy in him. There was no likeness to the man she had married. She expected someday he would not come home and there were days she thought that might not be a bad thing.

Her mind went back to the day she had given him the news.

She had been scared to tell him, having no idea how he would react to another child. Was it a good thing that would bring them closer together or would it push him further away. She remembered wrestling with this question for weeks once she became aware of the life within her. She had known she couldn't put it off much longer. Her belly was beginning to show. If he wasn't so withdrawn he would have noticed by now, she remembered thinking.

"I have news," she announced softly that day.

He had not lifted his eyes from the fire. His matted white hair had fallen forward around his head, covering most of his face.

She had moved across the mamateek and sat on the ground next to him.

She watched for a while as he idly scratched the ground with the short stick he was holding in his hand.

"I have news," she had repeated gently as she slipped her arm around his bent shoulders in an attempt to draw him back from the sad place he had gone.

She remembered him acknowledging her with a slight nod without looking up from the crackling fire in front of him.

Perhaps he isn't as far away as I believed, she had thought. Having gently taken his free hand in hers, she had then placed it on her belly. She had felt his shoulders stiffen under her arm.

"Yes, my husband, we are having a child," she'd whispered.

Unexpectedly he had begun to sob.

Wrapping her arms around her husband, Godabonyee had whispered, "It is a good thing, my husband."

"No," he'd sobbed, "it is not. There is nothing good about it."

"What do you mean?"

"There is no future for a child of ours."

"That's not true," she had said, feeling the stirring of uneasiness.

"This should never have happened," he had said a little more firmly. "There are no Beothuk left. What can a child of ours expect to do?"

"We will live as a family. That's all that matters."

"No. He will have to find a wife with the Buggishaman. Then there will be no place for him in Gossett with our ancestors. Is that what you want?"

"I don't care Langnon. This is my child and I will take care of it. Perhaps what we believe about Gossett is not true anyhow. Can you tell me it is?"

"Yes, Godabonyee. It is true. We have made a mistake here. You must find a way to rid yourself of it."

Godabonyee remembered how she had recoiled in shock. She was not prepared for this reaction. She was not about to let anything happen to this child. She had lost one, she wasn't going to lose another.

He lifted his head and his eyes had pierced into hers. "You will get rid of it or I will," he hissed at her.

She remembered pushing to her feet and hurrying to the door. Before stepping outside she looked back at her husband. He had gone back to staring into the fire and scratching on the ground with the stick.

She remembered placing her hand protectively over her belly and stepping through the opening, letting the caribou skin fall back into place. It had been days before she dared return to the mamateek.

Her mind had been a whirlwind of confusion that day as she wandered aimlessly through the woods. Surely he didn't want her to kill the child that lived inside her. That wasn't the Langnon she knew. How far down had the sadness dragged him? She knew he was living in a dark place of anger and despair but this was going too far. What was he thinking?

Sitting here across the fire from him, Godabonyee still wondered if the child were born would it be safe from him? She didn't think so.

Her thoughts returned to that day and how she had run from the clearing. She had wandered around the woods and without realizing it found her way to the hill overlooking the settlement. Finding a place to sit in the dry grass, she had looked out over the land that had been claimed by the Buggishaman.

She smiled as she remembered the scene that had been spread before her that evening. The sun was slipping behind the hills to her left and down below, lights had begun to flicker in the houses. In the distance she could see sails moving around the large harbour and on the shore Buggishaman were standing talking on the wharf. A horse drawn cart piled high with hay trundled along an uneven path between the Buggishaman's houses. Several small children ran behind it laughing and shouting happily.

She remembered it was the first time she had felt the baby move. It's too early, she had thought in dismissal, and lay back on the grass staring up at the faint clouds drifting across the darkening evening sky.

A plan had begun to form in her mind as she lay there.

She still had the winter to get through first.

Chapter 21

1832

That winter had been one of the longest she could remember. It seemed to drag by at a snail's pace. Langnon had spent much of his time in the other mamateek, surrounded by his lost son's memories. They seldom talked. They simply went through the motions of living.

There was very little snow left on the ground and the air was beginning to show signs of spring. The baby would come soon. Langnon had already made it clear he wanted no part of it. The line had been drawn and she was determined to take the side of the child. She would protect the baby at all cost.

Langnon had not been able to crawl back out of the hole he had fallen into. His deep sadness was often accompanied by times of dark anger. It seemed to Godabonyee that he was less and less able to control it and it worried her, even scaring her at times.

He had only beaten her a few times through the winter and she had been careful to protect the child. She knew he didn't mean to do it and he always cried and told her he was sorry afterwards. But she knew in her heart it would happen again.

The last of the ice had turned dark and melted in the harbour. The only remnant of winter was the iceberg that had found its way in from the open water of the bay. Most of the trees were now covered in buds and new growth was appearing everywhere. It was in this setting Godabonyee introduced her daughter to the world.

Godabonyee had left the mamateek early in the morning and made her way to the house of the Emamoose known as Manual. Langnon had been asleep in the other mamateek when she left the camp. She was careful not to wake him. He had already made it clear he did not want this baby. She still did not believe he would harm the child but she was not entirely sure. She had decided long ago she would not take the risk.

The baby made its entrance quietly. There was no loud yelling or screams of pain, just the strength and focus of two women who understood that the new life that was about to enter their world needed to be protected. They and the Emamooset were the only witnesses to her arrival.

Manual cleaned up the little one and handed her back to her mother. Godabonyee cradled her in her arm and studied her tiny face. She wanted to capture that picture in her mind to take with her when she left. She would never experience a moment like this again. There was a sadness that surrounded her yet she felt at peace leaving her with the Emamoose. Her baby would have a good life, better than she could provide for her. She would not know the ways of her parents and ancestors or speak their native tongue but she would have life; that was more important to Godabonyee. She would have a family. That was good enough.

Slowly, she lifted the swaddled baby from her chest and placed her in the outstretched arms of Manual as the Emamooset looked on.

Manual kissed the little baby's forehead, looked up at Godabonyee, and said, "Susannah."

"Susannah," repeated the Emamooset.

"Su-sann-naa," Godabonyee tried the word. She smiled at the Emamoose and nodded.

Brushing a tear from her eye, she gathered up her things and walked out the door, leaving behind the last true blood Beothuk to be born on the island.

All the way back to camp she wondered what her daughter would become, what she would be like when she grew. She wondered if the Emamoose would tell her who her mother was. She hoped so.

"Su-sann-naa." She liked how the name rolled. "Susannnaa."

Her mind turned to the reception she would get when she reached the camp. Langnon would probably be relieved that the baby was gone. She would never tell him the Emamoose had their baby. She would tell him it had died at birth.

She stooped and stepped through the door. He was sitting near the smoldering fire with his back to her.

"Where have you been?" he asked without turning around.

"At the river," she lied.

"Why?"

"The baby came."

"Where is it?" This time he turned and faced her.

"It did not live."

"Good."

She nodded silently.

"Now we can travel again."

"Where?"

"We are going back to the Great Lake. It is a good place to die. Our ancestors will be close to us there."

"When will we leave?" she asked, inwardly calculating how she could see her daughter one last time.

"Soon."

"That is a long trip. I need two days before I can travel."

"Two days then."

Before noon the next day she left the camp, heading for the coast. Deep in her shoulder bag she had secretly hidden the tiny moccasins she had made while Langnon slept in the other mamateek. She had not been able to find odemet so she used berry juice to stain them red. She thought it would probably be the last connection Susannnaa would have to her Beothuk roots so she wanted them to be made right.

Langnon had slept in the other mamateek again last night. She knew he would want to spend his last two nights there. She was surprised he had decided to leave it behind. She wondered if he would burn it before they left or would he try and take everything he could. Maybe now things would get better between them.

"Susannnaa," she kept repeating as she walked along the path that led to the Emamoose's place. She liked that name. She had an extra lightness in her step. She would get to see her daughter one last time.

Maybe this was not a good idea but she probably would never have this opportunity again. If they travelled all the way to the Great Lake they most likely would not return, at least not for years.

Once she was able to see the house through the trees she turned left and entered the woods. She made her way around the vegetable field until she reached the side of the house closest to the trees. The Buggishaman had been gone yesterday but he might be home now. She didn't want to be seen. She had said her goodbye and she just wanted to see her baby from a distance.

Godabonyee stood at the edge of the woods, hidden by a tall evergreen. She was close enough to the house to hear Susannnaa crying. The Emamoose was singing softly to her. She felt her heart flutter inside her chest.

Glancing down at the wharf, she noticed the Buggishaman's boat was still not there. Feeling safer, she crept to the side of the house and peeked through the cloudy glass of the single window.

Across the room near the stove, Manual sat in a rocking chair with Susannnaa cradled in her arms. Her head was bent over the baby as she gazed into her face and sang. The chair squeaked loudly each time she rocked.

Godabonyee could see her tiny face. It didn't matter that the glass distorted her vision a little, she was staring at the most beautiful little girl she had ever seen. "Susannnaa," she whispered softly.

She pulled back quickly as the Emamoose looked up and she slid down the wall to sit on the ground. Godabonyee sat there listening. She didn't understand the words but the sound was beautiful. She knew Susannnaa would be well taken care of. The realization that she would be safe now made her very happy. It made it a little easier to let her go.

She crept silently around the corner of the house and placed the tiny red moccasins on the step outside the door.

Quietly creeping back to her former position at the side of the house, she took one last peek through the window. She wanted to remember this scene forever. It would be all she had to carry with her through the next few years.

A smile crept across her face as she watched the two of them. Finally, she pushed away from the window and walked into the woods. The singing faded away behind her as she continued deeper into the forest.

As she drew closer to the camp she saw dark smoke billowing above the trees. It was more than the cooking fires would make. She quickened her step, ignoring the pain from her recent childbirth.

She thought about entering the clearing from the opposite side to the coast to hide the direction she was coming from but she was in a hurry. Stumbling into the clearing, she came to a stop next to a large boulder and stood there in surprise and fear. Langnon was pacing back and forth in front of the two burning mamateeks. It was easy to see he was in one of his rages. This was not good. She wondered what had triggered him to do this. She was scared.

He was muttering as he paced with his head down.

For a moment she considered backing into the woods and running, but she decided against it.

"Langnon, what have you done?" she asked timidly.

Seeing her there for the first time, he changed direction and strode purposefully across the clearing. His fists were curled at his side.

She took a step backwards until she felt her heel touch the base of the boulder.

He stopped with his face close to hers.

"Where were you?" he hissed.

"At the coast," she replied nervously, trying to avoid his fiery eyes.

"Don't lie to me. I know where you were. I saw you at the Buggishaman's house," he screamed at her.

His closed fist crashed into the side of her head and her legs buckled under her. She fell over backwards, hitting her head against the jagged edge of the boulder on the way down.

"Susannnaa," she whispered as the darkness closed in around her.

Langnon stood there watching her as she lay motionless on the ground. His arms hung at his sides. His fists were still tightly clenched. The dark thing that lived inside his head still had control of him, feeding his rage. Why had she gone to the Buggishaman? he wondered. He had warned her many times not to go there. Just like when she made him leave his family, she had to have it her way. It was always her way. She pushed him too much. She deserved to be hit.

He turned and looked over his shoulder at the blaze behind him. It was all gone. Everything was gone.

His eyes wandered back to the boulder, which now had a dark red streak across its face. His eyes then followed the blood stain down to the crumpled body of his wife beneath the rock. He felt strangely detached. It was as if he was standing outside this world looking in. He didn't belong here. There was no place for him anymore.

His tunic felt hot against his back, plastered to his body by the heat from the fiery mamateeks ablaze behind him. Already it was dying down, having quickly consumed everything. He stood there for a while and watched the flames flicker out until only glowing embers remained in the pile of ash.

Lifting his head toward the darkened sky, he felt the first drops of rain. He walked past the still form of Godabonyee and took the path toward the coast.

Jiggameel had come to him in a dream again last night. Just like before, he was standing just outside the mamateek holding the door flap partially open beckoning to Langnon to join him. As Langnon began to walk toward the door the flap began to fall into place. He broke into a run only to reach the door as the heavy flap completely covered the opening. He was not strong enough to push it back. Each time the dream came it ended the same way.

Langnon did not know what the dream meant or why his son always remained just out of reach but he believed Jiggameel was reaching out to him from beyond.

Thinking about the dream, he stumbled mindlessly along the trail that would lead him back to the coast. Birds fluttered around him. His moccasins squished loudly in the wet, muddy path, but he took no notice of any of it. He just continued walking until he came upon the hill where Jiggameel was lost.

Something had happened earlier today he knew but he couldn't remember. It seemed to have to do with Godabonyee. Somehow he sensed it was important but the memory could not seem to break through.

Seabirds swooped and dived in his direction as he disturbed them in his passing. He ignored them and found a place to sit on the ground in the midst of blackberry bushes loaded with ripe berries. The strong scent was overpowering. It seemed to temporarily clear his mind because all of a sudden the vivid picture of his son tumbling over the edge was all he could see. He looked around him. This was the place. He wondered how he got here. Where was Godabonyee?

Slowly the picture of Godabonyee's bloody head lying on the grass emerged from his clouded mind. Had he done that? he wondered.

Tiredly, he pushed to his feet, walked to the edge, and looked down at the jagged rocks where Jiggameel had lain. He wanted to be with his son again. Oddly, the fear that once would have paralyzed him standing this close to the edge was gone. He stared down through tired, watery eyes. Through his blurry vision he watched a doorway swing open to him.

He stepped off the edge.

Chapter 22
1853

"She's been asking for you."

With a heavy heart John hung his cap on the hook by the door and walked past Grace into the back room where his mother lay.

She had watched him row into the harbour he had no doubt. Her bed was arranged in front of the large window so she had a complete view of the harbour entrance. She had demanded it be that way once she had become too sick to get out of bed.

"I want to be able to see the comings and goings," she had said.

John had replaced the window with a larger one that extended almost to the floor. His eyes were always drawn to it every time he rounded the point and the house came into view.

A few years ago he had left the house he had grown up in with Sarah and moved into the new house he had built for himself and Grace. It was three coves away from Sarah's house but Grace liked it because it was a little closer to the bigger settlement and there were two families already living there.

Sarah had stayed on at the old house until she could no longer live on her own. The day he found her passed out on the floor of her kitchen in the midst of a pile of flour and half rolled dough is still etched in his mind. It seemed that she must have hit the table as she fell because he found it laying on its side.

He remembered running to her and shaking her until she opened her eyes. "I must have had a fainting spell," She said groggily.

That had been the beginning of it.

She had stayed in her home for nearly another full year until he found out the spells were becoming more frequent and would often come on with no warning. She reluctantly let him bring her to the new house.

"Tis only 'til I gets better," she had insisted as she climbed down the ladder into the dory. "I don't want to be no trouble."

"Yes mother," he had agreed, knowing it was the only way to get her out of there.

That was two years ago and she had never gone back. He had watched her steadily go downhill. The spells, as she referred to them, had gotten worse and now she was forgetting things;

simple things like her grandson's name. She often cried in frustration.

He hated seeing her this way and he knew it bothered William when she couldn't remember his name. He hadn't complained when he lost his bedroom to his grandmother. Often he would sit by her bedside and listen as she read aloud the stories she had read to his father so long ago.

Today she was alone in her room, propped up on her pillow, gazing out on the harbour. On her lap lay her bible opened to the family record page. He had seen that page many times before, though now it was worn with age and constant rifling. He remembered the day she had shown it to him for the first time and how it had made him feel part of her family. Next to the bible lay another smaller black leather-covered book. He had often seen her writing in it before but had never looked inside.

"Hi John," she said softly, without turning away from the window. "How were the fish today?"

"Good, Mother. How are you feeling?"

"I'm tired John. I just want to go with Andrew."

"You know I don't like it when you talk like that."

"I know John. Come sit by my side a while," she said, patting the wrinkled bed sheets.

John moved across the little room and took a seat in the chair next to her bed.

"John, there is something I want to show you," she said, turning to face him.

"What's that, Mother?"

"You know that those spells that have been troubling me have been happening more often these days. They last longer and sometimes they take things away from me."

John shook his head reassuringly but knew that what she was saying was true. Watching the familiar face that he had grown to love over the years, a feeling crept up on him that this could be one of the last times he would stare into his mother's eyes.

"I've been praying that they be taken away from me but it seems that is not going to happen. I know one of these days one of those spells will take me and I will not come out of it. That's alright with me, John. I don't want to be a burden on you and Grace anymore. When I go I will finally be with Andrew again, and I look forward to that."

John reached out and gently grasped her hand. "You have always been there for me ever since that day Andrew rescued me from the bear, and I will always be there for you. You are my mother, Sarah."

Sarah smiled at him through glistening eyes. "You were one prayer God answered for me, John. You have your own son now, and Grace. I couldn't have asked for a better son and I am so proud of you. That is why it is easy for me to let go."

She clasped her frail hands around the leather-bound book on her lap and held it out to John. "I want you to have this," she said.

"What is it?"

"It's your story, John. I wrote in there everything you told me about your people. I want you to take it. William will have children some day and he can pass it on to them. It will keep your story alive."

Three days later, John awoke to find Sarah lying on the old polar bear skin on the floor in her room. She never woke from what would be her final spell.

John took her back to their family home and buried her in the field behind the house. He had marked the grave with a simple wooden cross with her name, Sarah Foss, carved in the grain. There were now three crosses. Although Andrew's cross marked an empty grave John believed Sarah was finally reunited with him as she always wanted to be.

Slumped in his chair, John sat by the stove, staring at the berry-stained apron hanging on the hook by the door.

"Daddy, Nanny never finished the story she was reading me," said William, passing his father the ragged copy of Frankenstein.

"I'll finish reading you the book, William, but first let me read you a special story that Nanny left just for you."

John picked up the leather-bound book that sat on the table in front of him. He motioned for his son to sit in the chair next to him as he opened the cover to the first page.

"What is this story about, Daddy?" William asked.

"It's a story about you, and me. It's the story of our family and all our people. It's the story of the Red Indians."

Author's Notes

Susannah Manuel (1832 -1911) grew up in what would later become the town of Lewisporte in Notre Dame Bay. She would refer to her birth mother as Elizabeth.

She married Samuel Anstey (1832 – 1923).

In 1858 they had a daughter whom they named Mary (Mary Pond nee Anstey 1858 – 1895).

Shanawdithit spent five years in the service of John Peyton Jr. on Exploits Island, following which she was moved to St. John's. Her many conversations with William Cormack formed the base of most of our recorded history of the Beothuk. She died there on June 6, 1829 under the care of Dr. William Carson. Like so many of her tribe, it was the Buggishaman's "coughing disease" that finally took her to be with her ancestors. Sometimes on a clear night, if you look real close, you just might see her star high over the South Side hills in St. John's.

Natural history presents itself in a vague and impersonal way, devoid of color or character, leaving the reader with facts and truth but not of the individual and the life they lived. In this series of books, I have strived to rectify that injustice by introducing you to some of these forgotten people and hopefully creating a picture of their lives lived.

Success, although often lacking a reliable yardstick, might be measured when we happen to meet on the street and our conversation turns to Shanadee and the plight of her lost family.

Glossary of Terms

The following represents a list of Beothuk words used in this book. These were provided to William Cormack by Shanawdithit during their many conversations.

Buggishaman	*white man*
Emamoose	*white woman*
Emamooset	*white girl*
Gossett	*land of the dead*
Hathemay	*bow*
Moisamadrook	*wolf*
Monau	*seal*
Odemet	*red ochre*
Tapaithook	*canoe*
Washawet	*bear*

<u>Locations</u>

The Great Lake	*Red Indian Lake*
The Great River	*Exploits River*

Historical Characters

A number of historical characters are represented in this book. As a work of historical fiction, fictional characters are used to develop a picture of the missing pieces and stories of what the lives of these historical characters might have been.

Terry's Books

<u>*The Red Indian series:*</u>

Red Indian – The Early Years: published March 2015.

This, the first book in the series, follows the lives of Shanawdithit's mother, Shanadee, and her family as they struggle to survive the formidable challenges mounted against them by the arrival of the early European settlers to the shores of Newfoundland.

Red Indian – The Final Days: published March 2016.

The second book in the series brings the stories of the fifteen Beothuk that Shanawdithit reported to William Cormack were living at the time she was captured. It attempts to provide some insight into what may have happened to them as they disappeared.

Red Indian – The Beginning: published July 2017.

Having no access to pen and paper, the Beothuk passed on the stories of their families by word of mouth. The third book in this series records the stories of the ancestors of Shanadee and Kirradittii, as told so many times around the family campfire.

Bloody Point: published July 2019.

Legend has it that Hants Harbour, a small community on the eastern shore of the island of Newfoundland, was the scene of a terrible Beothuk massacre of unprecedented scale. Although history is vague on the facts, and the numbers may have possibly been exaggerated, there are those who still relate the story with conviction.

Beothuk Slaves: published October 2020.

Following a failed attempt in 1500, Portuguese explorer Gaspar Corte Real, landed on the island of Newfoundland. He captured fifty-seven Beothuk and sent them back to Portugal on two of his accompanying ships. Gaspar remained to further explore. He was never heard of again. This is how I imagine the end of his story.

Holmes: published July 2022.

Seasonal fishermen dared not venture to the southern side of Fogo Island for fear of an encounter with the Beothuk. That was before John Holmes. In 1823 he took the chance and set up tilts in Seldom Come By. Five years later he became its first permanent settler. This is his story.

Through Beothuk Land: published July 2025

The year was 1822. The Beothuk population was now reduced to a few. William Epps Cormack launched an expedition to find any surviving members of the Beothuk nation. In his search, Cormack, with his young Mi'kmaq guide, walked across the interior of the island of Newfoundland. This book takes you along on this harrowing journey.

For information on Terry's published books as well as future books, please take a moment to "like" and follow Terry Foss Author Facebook page or visit Terry's website shown below.

Website: www.terryfoss.ca

Email: terryfoss@nf.sympatico.ca

Facebook: facebook.com/terryfossauthor

Distribution: www.shopdownhome.com

www.ingramcontent.com/pod-product-compliance
Lightning Source LLC
Chambersburg PA
CBHW060526260626
47161CB00003B/784
* 9 7 8 0 9 9 4 0 2 0 9 2 5 *